THE LAST PROPHET

THE LAST PROPHET

Sidney Weinstein

iUniverse, Inc.
New York Lincoln Shanghai

The Last Prophet

Copyright © 2006 by Sidney Weinstein

iUniverse books may be ordered through booksellers or by contacting:

iUniverse
2021 Pine Lake Road, Suite 100
Lincoln, NE 68512
www.iuniverse.com
1-800-Authors (1-800-288-4677)

ISBN-13: 978-0-595-40095-9 (pbk)
ISBN-13: 978-0-595-84479-1 (ebk)
ISBN-10: 0-595-40095-7 (pbk)
ISBN-10: 0-595-84479-0 (ebk)

Printed in the United States of America

PART I

CHAPTER 1

▼

In the year 1995, Joseph Stern, an eighteen-year-old youth was in a deep sleep. In the blackness of that night and in a vivid dream, he heard a deep resonant voice speak to him. The words had the impact of hammer blows and .he writhed as he heard them. "Joseph, Joseph,"came the voice. "You have been gifted with the prophecy of truth. Go forth and prophesy the truth throughout the land". In his dream and trembling with fear, Joseph called out." How do I do this?" The voice reverberated "Go forth, Joseph," and trailed off, "Joseph, go forth." Joseph woke up, trembling, soaked with perspiration. His mind racing with the impact of that dream. What did it mean? Was this an edict from a celestial being? Why this strange and compelling emotion that he must obey and fulfill the message of that dream. These thoughts and myriad others plagued him the rest of the night until the dawn came announcing a new day.

Joseph got up and dressed. It was the day after his graduation from High School. That had been a day filled with much activity and many plaudits for his scholastic work and his role as class president. He came from a good family with loving parents who beamed with pride at their son's many accomplishments. Joseph had plans to attend a first rate university with studies that could lead to a career in journalism or political science. Now his mind was in turmoil caused by the message in his dream. That message was becoming an obsession that gave him no rest.

Joseph decided to seek advice and discuss his problem with others. His first choice was school counselor, Mr.Stevens. A warm friendly confidant.Mr.Stevens greeted him and waved him to a chair. He said, "Joseph, good to see you. You are leaving us, but we know you will do well and we are very proud of you." Joseph thanked him, seated himself, then divulged his dream and its effect on him. Finishing he looked up. With his hands clasped in front of him, Mr.Stevens listened intently, a serious expression on his face. After a lengthy pause, he spoke. "Joseph, evidently this dream has had a deep and troubling effect on you. Has there been any event or experience of reading, studies or other factors that could have originated the basis for this dream?" Joseph thought, then shook his head, "No," he replied, "Nothing like that." Mr.Stevens continued, "In the Old Testament, Joseph, your namesake, the son of Jacob, was gifted with the ability to interpret prophetic dreams. A gift that gave him great power and influence. Perhaps a subconscious recall of that ancient biblical event has created the substance of that dream and given it the image of reality." As Joseph moved uneasily in his chair, Mr.Stevens studied him in silence and then spoke. "Joseph, you are a brilliant student with the ability and character to be a success in any career you choose. You can become a civic leader to help achieve the best in our society. Put aside this disturbing dream. It is just an incomprehensible emanation of brain activity during its period of sleep rejuvenation. Think only of the reality of daily living and of the challenges and obstacles to be met and overcome." Mr.Stevens sat back and waited for his answer.

Joseph was slow to respond. Finally, voice trembling he began. "I don't know how to say this, but that dream has changed me. A door opened inside me and I was in a new space. I have always felt different in the way I saw things. All about me I see lies, injustice and hate. Hate and violence are widespread. People preach love and practice hate. The dream told me, "Go Forth." I don't know how, or where, or what I can do. But, I cannot help myself. Perhaps losing friends, family, and everything else. I must go, I can.t stop it. I must go." He stopped and, burst into tears with deep sobs and heaving chest. Mr.Steven got up and walked to him. He put his arms around him and held him until his sobbing stopped. Then he helped him to his feet and walked him to the exit.

The next day, Joseph decided to have a discussion with his parents. In the evening, after dinner, he advised them he needed to have an important discussion with them. Impressed by his serious demeanor, they readily agreed. After the table was cleared, they gathered in the den.

Following a period of silence, Joseph began and related his dream and the overwhelming effect it had on him. That it now was changing his plans for his future. His parents listened with unbelieving astonishment. When Joseph finished, there was a period of intense silence. Finally, his father spoke, "Joseph, I respect your feelings. You know how proud we are of you and your outstanding scholastic and other school activities and achievements. You know our desires for your success and happiness. Now we hear you say that because of a very vivid and disturbing dream you are preparing to discard everything.

"Your education, career, friends, family, a promising future. All this for a dream, a fantasy, an ephemeral vision of a future, confusing and wrapped in uncertainties. As your parents, who love you and want your life to be productive and happy, we entreat you.

"Put aside this momentary intrusion into the normal progress of your life." He stopped and then his mother spoke. "Joseph, listen to your father. He has gained much wisdom in his life and what he tells you is based on many years experience. We both have only your interest at heart and speak to you from the depths of our love for you. Heed your father's advice. It will prove best for you." She finished and they both studied Joseph for his reply.

Joseph spoke after a brief moment. "This is very difficult for me. I am talking about a dream. Not physical, not real, not substantial and yet so powerful that it has created an obsession that commands me to follow a message. No matter where it leads. I have tried to deny it, but have failed. I have tried to forget it, I cannot. I have told myself I will not do it, but feel I must. I am no longer in control of myself, but have become the instrument of something else. Is this a command from God? All my thinking and philosophy rejects that idea. The voice in my dream said, "Go forth and disclose the truth throughout the land." The words: "Go Forth" keep ringing in my mind obscuring all else. What am I to do? How do I begin? Joseph stopped and cupped his head in his hands, obviously distraught. His parents observed him with concern. His father then asked, "What are your immediate plans? You have been admitted to Slocum University, Will you be taking your courses as planned?" Joseph replied, "No, I am considering not attending." His father shook his head. "Joseph, your tuition has been paid. I urge you to attend. I don't want to impose. You did express doubts on how to proceed on this new venture. Get yourself some breathing space. Attend college and let time resolve your dilemma. I don't like to set conditions, but if you promise to attend college will accept and support any future decision you make regarding your lifestyle." Joseph pondered this statement for some time and then spoke, "Dad, with all respect and since I don't know what else to do, I will comply with your request. I promise to begin my studies and hope that time will disclose the road I am to travel." With a sigh of relief, the father clasped the hand of his wife and broke into a smile.

CHAPTER 2

▼

The following week was a period of activity as Joseph prepared to leave for his university. When that day arrived, Joseph departed, leaving behind a tearful mother and a caring father. As he hugged him, his father said, "Be strong, be righteous."

Upon entering the university campus, Joseph found himself in the company of many new students. A very congenial group with whom Joseph quickly established a warm relationship. They were all eager to help one another. They were all anxious to share their feelings about this advent into a major educational experience. Assigned to a dormitory, Joseph found he was to share it with another new student. His name, Jack Winton, was a tall, lanky, western type from Montana. Laconic in speech and very agreeable to Joseph. They quickly reached agreement on bed, locker, and desk space in their sparse quarters. There was no TV or radio in the room. Items they both agreed would interfere with their studies. They busied themselves arranging their personal belongings, preparing for their first class, starting on the morrow.

That morning, the freshmen were assembled in the auditorium to be welcomed by the Dean and faculty members. The Dean spoke of the purpose and traditions of the University. That the University existed to help them expand their knowledge and intellect. To assist all students in achieving skills and professional abilities needed for their chosen careers. That each of you will become a contrbutor to a better society for all your fellow citizens. In return, we desire that you cherish this, your new home of learning. Honor and respect its traditions, and seek by your conduct to add luster to its reputation. His closing salutation was greeted by loud and sustained applause.

Leaving the auditorium, Joseph and his roommate entered their first classroom. They took their seats, as preferred, in the rear row. The subject, history was taught by Professor Ralph Williams. Professor Williams was a graduate from a prominent Eastern university and possesed many degrees. He had a reputation as a militant activist. As Professor Williams entered the room, the students respectfully rose to their feet. Professor Williams acknowledged the gesture, and with a wave of his hand, signalled them to be seated. A tall lean man, he was dressed in a careless manner. Open sport shirt, jean trousers, and tennis shoes. He sported a slight beard, unruly hair and an intense and energetic expression. His voice, when he spoke, was clear and forceful. He began, by welcoming the students, and then launched into a description of their studies of history. He announced, "We will begin with the study of American history. We will be looking at history as it is written. Keeping in mind, that history is written by the victors and fashioned on their triumphs. Our studies will search the underlying realities that have been glossed over by noble words that conceal agendas not noble but often contrary.

"An example is the Pilgrims landing on our shores, in 1620. They came, as recorded, in search of religious freedom. It was not as generally accepted, religious freedom for all religions, considered the basis for our current doctrine of separation of church and state. They sought religious freedom for only their religion and had no tolerance for other faiths." Following these remarks, Professor Williams turned to his notes and gave the class reading assignments for the next class session.

After the evening meal, Joseph and his roommate Jack began a study period. Concentrating on their studies, they engaged in no conversation. Much later they called a halt to their studies and prepared for bed. Jack took out a Bible and spent a short time reading it. Finishing, he turned to Joseph and said. "I don't know how you feel about using the Bible, but if you choose, you are welcome to use it." Joseph thanked him and replied, "I appreciate your offer but I believe your bible is the New Testament. I am Jewish and my religion only accepts the Old Testament on which your Bible is based." Jack expressed surprise. "I have never met a Jew and thought everyone accepted the teachings of this Bible. What is there in it you don't accept?" Joseph responded, "Many of your Bible teachings are the same as ours. However, my religion forbids believing a human can be or is a God. We also believe that life after death is unknowable and incomprehensible to humans. So we have no doctrine on a heaven or a hell. We are only to be concerned with the life given here on earth. That all human life is sacred and we are to be judged by our deeds, not our faith. The moral values ordained by our Ten Commandments are acknowledged by most religions.

Jack said, "I am puzzled. If you don't believe in a hereafter, what is the purpose of our life? Does it mean, we are here today and gone tomorrow? That is all it is? That God has given us brains, talent, will and intelligence to be dumped at the end of physical life? It doesn't make sense." Joseph nodded his head, "I agree. Greater minds than ours have debated this question for centuries with no credible answer. So it comes down to faith and belief in the unprovable. My religion informs that since this matter is beyond human resolution, we should not burden ourselves with its incomprehensible mystery. That this is the area and responsibility of divine authority and our duty is to make a good life for ourselves and our fellow human beings here on this earth we all share. Jack heaved a sigh, "Well, on that heavy note, let's hit the hay." Saying "good night," the lights were turned off.

The next morning, after breakfast in the cafeteria, Jack and Joseph entered their next subject classroom. The subject was sociology and was taught by professor Don Hayden.

Professor Hayden was a medium size man, in his late 50's, with black graying hair, and a ruddy complexion. He was dressed neatly and wore a tie. His approach to the students was jovial and he opened the lecture with a joke. The subtlety of the joke escaped most of the students and only a few responded with laughter. He followed this with some personal questions obviously trying to familiarize himself with the students and to establish rapport with them. He then turned his attention to the subject. "Sociology," he declared, "is the study of human society and the ingredients of its composition and behavior patterns. Remember," he added, "The human is an animal and its beginning of culture and social grouping has its source in animal behavior. A study of the close bonding of the grey wolves family enclave gives a clue to how the human family bonding expanded to the human tribal bonding. While the progression of civilization diminished many of the animal qualities of the humans, many of the animal qualities persisted to the detriment of civilized progress." The class ended with a discussion of these factors raised by the lecture.

Later in afternoon, Jack and Joseph decided to do some study in the study lounge, a large, well lit room with ample chairs and table space. After an hour or so of study, they were distracted by the entry of five students, two male and three female students. Who greeted them warmly and after informal introductions, were invited to join them. Happy to escape the dullness of study and to enjoy a bit of light socializations, they shut their books and joined the group; these were very vivacious people. The conversation covered a variety of topics with much laughter particularly when discussing some of the personal idiosyncrasies of their professors and classroom humorous incidents. They discussed movies, TV shows, music and funny back-home events. Serious subjects received only cursory mention and the hilarity of the occasion achieved a welcome pause to the burden of scholastic effort. The men, Bob medium size with an athletic build, blonde hair, and Peter, tall, thin, slightly balding and wearing glasses. Both outgoing with a good sense of humor. The women were all slim and attractive. Mallory a very attractive young lady had credentials as a top student, with a quick facile mind and who laughed a lot. Megan had a Tahiti background and also a top student with a very happy attitude. Allison, with a stunning figure was a top-scoring woman athlete and a honor student as well. Jack and Joseph enjoyed this group although their participation was limited. When Allison asked Joseph why he had so little to say, embarrassed, he replied, "I am not very good at small talk." Allison advised, "Small talk is what keeps the machinery of society moving." With a wry smile, Joseph responded, "I guess you are right." Evidencing interest in Joseph, Allison questioned further, "Well, what major topics do you discuss?" Pleased and flattered by her interest, Joseph responded. "Perhaps I am overly concerned but I feel, the human race is on a path of self-destruction." Allison smiled." Does Joseph plan to save us," Joseph replied, "History tells us that earth shaking movements were often started by one individual. Perhaps, events will produce such a leader who will bring sanity to our existence." Allison said, "You are a very profound young man. We are attending a demonstration this evening on the despoiling of the environment, which you might like to attend and which fits your serious concerns." Joseph thanked her for the invitation, said he would plan on attending and be looking forward to future conversations with her. Saying their farewells, Jack and Joseph left for their room.

That evening, desiring another meeting with Allison and curious as to the planned demonstration, Joseph decided to attend. He asked Jack to join him, but Jack declined saying that he needed to catch up on his studies. So Joseph went alone. The demonstration was taking place in front of a large terrace at the entry to the Slocum auditorium. On the terrace facing the large grassy field, a speaker dais with microphone faced the audience assembling there. Several large banners with big letters proclaiming "Save Our Environment" established the purpose of the demonstration. The ceremony was scheduled to start at 7 P.M. and by 6:50 about 1500 students had filled the field. Joseph had arrived at that time and eagerly searched the crowd for Allison but was unable to locate her. He finally gave up and concentrated on the dais where the speakers were assembled. Joseph recognized Professor Williams who appeard to be their leader. Two of the members were obviously students and two others, a middle aged, well-dressed woman and an elderly distinguished looking man. Promptly at seven, Professor Williams stepped to the microphone and calling for quiet, declared the meeting opened. He then stated in a loud, clear voice, "Students and honored guests, we are gathered this evening to express concern for increasing destruction of our environment and species. But first, I will introduce the panel members present: Our senior student class president, Phillip Haber. Our school publication editor, student Frank Willard, noted author, journalist, and world affairs pundit, Robert Cundall, and the distinguished Senator from our State, Charlotte Ardeth, well known nationally and internationally. These and many others have joined us in our cause that protests the environmental destruction that lays waste the fertile regions of the earth and turns it into desert. A desert bordered by oceans, once teeming with living species that supported life being transformed into a poisonous fluid unfit for life or life enjoyment. How to resolve this dilemma? How to reverse this destructive trend and restore the self-healing forces of nature? Is it too late? Have we passed the point of no return? With these meetings, we seek answers to difficult questions. We seek your help as well as from others. We will now hear from Student Phillip Haber, Senior Class President." The audience responded with heavy applause. After adjusting the microphone, student Haber spoke, "When my grandparents lived in Ohio, the State was covered with hardwood forests that in autumn turned into a colorama with leaves of gold, yellow, red, and brown forest spectacle. Rivers of crystal pure water flowed between banks of lush green vegetation. The pure untainted air was filled with the sound and song of birds. The land I will bequeath to my future descendents will be different. It will be filled, not with the glory of nature's rivers and forests, but with man made concrete highways, man made structures, and air and rivers polluted with man made industrial and human waste. To my future descendents, please accept my deep and sorrowful apology for the failure of we humans to recognize that we are part of a cosmic plan that all life is woven into. That human arrogance that despoils everything in pursuit of selfish, greedy objectives destroys the harmony of the universe and in the end our survival." He finished and bowed in response to loud applause.

Professor Williams then introduced Frank Willard, the school paper editor, who held up his hands in greeting and then spoke." As students we are told we can change the world, and change it for the better. That is quite a challenge since we will be busy, earning a living, fostering our careers, striving to establish a family. What priority does changing the world, command? In our lifetime, it may not be too relevant. But as Willard said, the world we leave our descendents is terribly important. Our planet is in distress. Each decade, brings additional destruction to the environment. We must all unite in this fatal struggle to save our planet." He stopped and shouted, "SOP, Save Our Planet" The audience rose to its feet and applauding, shouted, "SOP."

Professor Williams stepped to the microphone acquiring quiet, introduced the next speaker, Robert Cundall. He gave a brief description of his eminent career and of his having written extensively on environment, as a journalist who covered world affairs, and was frequently consulted on current events. Acknowledging with humility, the glowing introduction, and in a quiet but clear voice Cundall addressed the audience. "Fellow Americans, I have spent a large portion of my life and energy to avoid the impending sentence of doom threatening life on this planet unless we reverse the current destruction of our living environment. But reversing this trend is extremely difficult because it does not involve overcoming physical and tangible objects, but an abstract factor that resists change. That obstacle is the human mind. The human mind is motivated by a desire for immediate material and political benefits, disregarding future resulting consequences that will bring disaster. How does one change a mind-set that refuses to accept the road to survival? We cannot change human nature that denies reality. In my judgement, our only positive approach is to have governments take up our cause and pass laws that will reverse current destructive trends. These laws would encourage the production of non-polluting replacement fuel for oil, protect endangered species. Stop the destruction of Brazilian rain forests. A major source of oxygen replenishment and absorbtion of carbon dioxide, as well as a reservoir of unidentified plants that may contain unknown substances vital for curing disease. The clearing of these forests provides farmland with soil unsuited for farm produce.

"To accomplish this, we must unite and activate our communities to the need for legislative action. Our government must assume a leadership role in reversing environmental destruction. You students, who represent our future leaders, must become warriors in this war against ignorance, stupidity, greed, and self interest, and fight for our survival and the heritage we leave our children." He shouted "Save our planet," and sat down. The audience rose to its feet and gave him a long-standing ovation.

After an interval, Professor Williams raised his hand for quiet and introduced the next speaker. "Our next speaker needs no introduction, since her frequent appearances on television has made her known throughout the nation and the world. Senator Charlotte Ardeth has been a very strong advocate of environmental protection, and has been responsible for several laws protecting the environment. She has been a cosponsor of the Ardeth-Long bill that set aside a large wilderness area as an endangered wild life refuge. She is one of the most popular member of the Senate. She has taken time off from her busy senate duties to speak to us, because this topic is so important to her. It now gives me great pleasure to introduce Senator Ardeth." The audience responded by rising to their feet with heavy applause. Smiling, Senator Ardeth accepted the applause. A trim, middle age attractive woman with red hair, she waited intil the applause subsided and then spoke in a clear, forceful voice. "Dear students, faculty members and honored guest. As a former student, like you I stood at the threshold of life. Eager to test myself in that adventure but filled with trepidation as to my ability to attain my goals. What was in store for me? Will I achieve self-sufficiency, family, career? I know those same questions trouble you. That earning the approval of your family and your responsibility to society burden your mind. Be of good cheer. With confidence in your ability and focusing all your energy in a positive direction, all things are possible and the future becomes secure. My own career exemplifies the opportunities for success in this open and free society that we have. Now I would like to address the problem we have met to discuss. Being in the legislature of the world's most powerful nation, I am keenly aware that we can enact laws that will preserve our wilderness areas, reduce or eliminate pollution, protect endangered species. Together, I with like thinking colleagues, have struggled to effect such measures. Our major obstacles are the large corporations that spend huge sums influencing legislators to protect the economic well-being of their corporations. Time and time again, we have seen standards for eliminating industrial and auto pollution lowerd or eliminated in order to favor corporate financial interests. A glimmer of hope is that dwindling energy sources will force the development of renewable non-polluting energy sources and away from the disappearing oil products.

As an individual, you may feel helpless and ineffective in the sweep of national and world events. There is something you can do that may have results, and that is to actively support our efforts. Do that by educating all you meet and know to the gravity of our present situation. Best of all let your representatives in Congress know your strong sentiments. They are sensitive to the demands of their voters and influenced by it. Heavy volume on a particular subject can have a decisive effect on a legislator's vote. In closing, I urge you to be strong and active in support of our goals. Thank you." She finished and bowed in recognition of a standing ovation.

Professor Williams took the stand and thanked the Senator for her attendance. He then asked the audience to participate with questions and opinions. He stated a traveling attendant would provide a microphone to those speaking and asked that they give their name and status when recognized. In response many hands were raised and Professor Williams chose the speaker by pointing his hand and describing his choice. After securing the microphone, the individual selected declared, "I am Steven Cooper, a senior student and my concern is global warming that will cause the polar caps to melt inundating coastal areas by rising oceans. Enviromentalist claim human pollution is the cause but some scientist disagree and say these are normal weather cycles and point to the ice age as proof. Who is right? Perhaps Mr. Cundall can answer that question." Robert Cundall took the stand and replied, "That is an excellent question and I am happy to respond to it. There is no doubt that human pollution is causing a dramatic climatic change. The theory that explains the ice age is that it was not a normal weather cycle but one caused by a collision with this planet of a huge meteor that raised a cloud of dust that enveloped the earth and completely blotted out the sun's warming rays for several years causing the formation of huge glaciers that covered the earth. The current pollution affecting our climate is no accident but a deliberate process." The next student recognized also poised a question for Mr.Cundall. He said, "I am Cecil Gorman, a second year student, and I wonder about the Endangered Species Act. I can understand protecting large and noteworthy creatures, but some seem so insignificant with little role in the environment yet large areas are set aside for their protection. Do they have an importance, not obvious?" Cundall responded, "In the cosmic plan of nature's organization all life is interrelated. Species we thought irrelevant were later found to be part of a chain of life that maintains the complicated and fragile balance of nature. Every orgasnism no matter how insignificant plays a part, not obvious, in the fantastic panorama of nature's scenario. Our duty is to preserve all species, not injurias to man, from extinction." He finished, then Professor Williams recognized another student, who was Joseph. Joseph rose to his feet, he rejected the microphone offered to him and turning towards the audience spoke out. "I am Joseph Stern, a freshman student"

Speaking without a microphone, his voice rang out loud and clear to the furthest portion of his audience. His voice carried a resonance; a musical timbre, a warmth of passion that immediately captivated all attending. In rapt silence they listened intently as his words packed with the intensity of his emotion rang out with such harmonious sounds that some would compare it to opera. He declared, "In all this discussion of environment. I have not heard one word of what I consider the primary cause of its destruction. That is the uncontrolled over-population of our planet. The current census gives the world's human population as six billion. The projected population in some forty years is stated as ten billion. Our planet can probably support a population, with an acceptable standard of living, of about three billion. The planet resources cannot support a population in excess of that number. Fertile land needed for food production is being covered with concrete and buildings, rivers and oceans that provide us essential food are being polluted. A population of billions lives in squalor, poverty, and ignorance. Ruled by corrupt dictators, their only production is large numbers of unneeded and deprived children. Doomed to a hopeless life and subject to disease, malnutrition, and violence, their existence is in constant peril. I ask the panel, how can this problem be addressed?"

There was a long pause, while the panel discussed the answer to the question. Finally Professor Williams spoke. "Joseph, you have broached a root question that underlines the whole question of environmental protection. There is no doubt that over-population is the chief cause of environmental problems. How to curb and reverse it is very complex and difficult. It involves human behavior and a change in human thinking and behavior. Changing human behavior is the most difficult of all tasks. It involves religion, tradition, politics, family, tribal and social norms. Frankly, I am at loss as to what aproach would be effective, so will implore, Robert Cundall whose world experience may better suit him, for a reply." Cundall assumed the microphone and said, "I trust Professor Williams will not be disappointed in his misplaced confidence as to my ability to answer this very difficult question. But will try. The only proven effective measures that can reverse this trend are threefold. First-the world must condemn violence that helps keep brutal and corrupt regimes in power. Second-It must force nations to give women equal rights and control of their bodies. Thirdly-Promote education based on human rights and democratic principles. The birth rate in the democratic nations with human and womens' rights has diminished to a very low point. While the underveloped and undemocratic nations have excessive birth rate. This is a difficult but effective program Thank you." and sat down to applause. Professor Williams thanked him and said, "As usual, Robert, you have exceeded my expectations." This was followed by a salvo of questions that the panel sought to answer. Having called for a final question, Professor Williams announced, the time was late and declared the meeting ended. As the group disbanded, Joseph was pleasantly surprised to be confronted by Allison, who had searched him out. She extended her hand in congratulations on the importance of his statement and question. She said, "I see you have no problem speaking out when you have something important to say. I was quite impressed by the knowledge and insight of your remarks." Joseph replied, "When I arrived I looked but was unable to locate you. I am so pleased we have met again." At this Allison favored him with a smile. Encouraged, Joseph invited her to join him for a soft drink at a nearby ice cream parlor. She agreed, and soon they were seated comfortably in a booth and enjoying their drink. Allison remarked, "When we first met, I thought you attractive, but shy and not too bright. Tonight I realized that you are intelligent, profound can speak out boldly and quiet charismatic. You are truly an enigma and I wonder what other secret qualities you conceal." Joseph responded, "I am gratified and flattered by your mistaken high esteem. I am a mediocre person suffering from the same feelings of inadequancies and unworthiness that most young people feel. I do have a deep concern for matters affecting our lives and society which enables me to speak out forcefully on these concerns.

You are a beautiful, intelligent, charming young lady and I feel honored by your kind attention." Allison smiled and said, "I enjoy talking with you and look forward to future meetings." Joseph was silent, he looked into her eyes with a serious expression and after a long pause, he said, "Allison, I am going to propose something and if you disapprove, please do not hesitate to express your disapproval." With a puzzled expression she studied him. Joseph continued. "Everyone needs a confidant, someone who will listen, not necessarily to give advice, but just to give ear to the burden someone carries. I carry such a burden, one that gives me much anxiety and mental turmoil." He paused and tears glistened in his eyes. "I need such a confidant to help ease the burden I carry, alone. Dear Allison, I thought of you. Although we met briefly, I felt comfortable in your presence and that you are one, to whom, I could, freely express my problem. I know this is presumptive, and will willingly accept your refusal." He stopped and looked at her, searching for her answer. Allison paused and then asked, "I am curious as to why you select a woman as your confidant. Wouldn't a man be more suitable for a man's problems?" Joseph replied, "Yes, for subjects usual for mens concerns, women, marriage, sex, business, sports, male activities, finance. My problem is in a different category and cannot be considered by male macho thinking but requires the sensitive and understanding nature of the feminine mind. I feel you have the qualities I need in a confidant." Allison reached over and took Joseph's hand in hers. Looking intently into his face, said, "I would be honored to be your friend and confidant." Overjoyed Joseph raised her hand to his lips and thanked her. "Joseph," Allison said, "If you want to talk now, I will listen. Joseph shook his head. "The hour is late and I better walk you back. Before I talk, we should get to know each other better. I will want to see you again soon." Allison agreed and they both got up together and left. After leaving Allison at her dormitory, Joseph headed back to his residence. His path took him through an area thickly lined with trees. He felt elated by the results of his meeting with Allison. For the first time, felt the driving force of his "go forth" message muted by the experience of that meeting. As he walked, his mind sought to analyse this new feeling of relief. A sudden blast of wind filled the air and whistled shrilly through the treetops. The air was filled with shrieking sound. The noise interrupted Joseph's thoughts. Suddenly he froze and listened in terror. Within the clamoring noise of the wind, he thought he heard his name called repeatedly. In trembling fear, he screamed, "What is it? What do you want?" he heard no answer. The wind abated and was replaced by calm. Distraught, his mind in turmoil, Joseph resumed his walk and reached his dormitory. Entering his roon, Jack greeted him and asked, "How was it?" Joseph answered, "Interesting," and prepared for bed.

CHAPTER 3

▼

At night as he tried to sleep, he felt disturbed by the message still burning within him. He couldn't shut out the sound of the voices he thought were calling to him from out of the wind. They had penetrated with violence into his being. He tried to recreate within his mind the sound of his name he believed he heard. Was he going crazy? Was false fantasy imagination taking hold of him? Did he really hear voices? He thought of the many religious leaders who claimed to have had conversations with God, and their many followers that believed them. He had felt ridicule for them as false charlatans who did this to gain control and profit from gullible followers. Was he becoming like them in claiming communication with spiritual sources? All his realistic and prosaic thinking rebelled at that idea. And yet, that he was experiencing forces beyond normal human senses was becoming very real to him. Controlled by incomprehensible forces, he felt lonely and adrift. He tossed and turned most of the night, his mind spinning through events of the past turbulent week as he sought to escape the troubling events and find sleep. His thoughts turned to Allison and she came to him as a warm glowing light shedding warmth into the cold recesses of his troubling thoughts. How beautiful she is, how good, kind and sweet, how intelligent. And she likes me, he was sure. Wrapped in this memory, Joseph relaxed and finally fell asleep. The following morning, after little sleep, Joseph was awakened by Jack, "Get up.we will be late for our morning class." After a hasty breakfast, Joseph still drowsy, they reported to Professor Williams's class. The subject, early American history, dealt with the early settlements of English colonists. Professor Williams defined how the early settlers were welcomed by the native Indians. But as their numbers grew and they established private ownership of land, their warmth turned to hostility. Owning land was a concept inconceivable to them. They could not comprehend private, restrictive ownership of land that belonged to the Great Spirit. As conflict between British and French for territorial control grew, the Indians were recruited by both sides for war against the other. Massacre of inhabitants was a warfare practice of Indians, and both sides were its victims. Out of this chaos, the original English colonies were established. English success in war forced peace upon the Indians, and their forced acceptance of colonies on their land. Professor Williams stated that in examining these historical events, they must understand that the principles of morality and justice were irrelevant to those following the beliefs of "Manifest Destiny." The discussion that followed was lively with most of the class involved. The session ended as Professor Williams complimented them on their active participation. Dismissing the class, he asked Joseph to remain. The class left, leaving Joseph alone with the professor. He offered Joseph a seat close to his desk and then spoke. "Joseph, at our meeting last evening you spoke out with a question that was most intelligent and discerning. Your voice and manner of speaking immediately commanded everyone's attention. You evidently are gifted with oratorical qualities as well as a profound insight into current problems of our society. There are all too few young people who possess these qualities. My reason for this interview is to have you, if you choose, become an active member of an organization I helped start. This organization is called *Pioneers of the Future* and its purpose may suit your concerns. We hope to reverse the destructive trends of human behavior that are destroying our planet. Our goal is to eliminate violence, war, poverty and ignorance and bring the blessing of peace to all people. University students have been the catalyst for beneficial change in some nations. We need gifted young student speakers, like you, to marshal large numbers of students to our cause. Joseph, give my request serious consideration and if you are deeply concerned about the current situation remember that anger, outrage, frustration are ineffectual unless they lead to positive action. Take your time, I will await your reply."

Joseph bowed his head and frowned in deep thought. Is this he wondered a road opening for him that would enable him to deliver his message? Why was he being selected? He felt powerful forces surging within him that made it difficult for him to breathe. Finally, able to control himself, he said, "I don't know how suited I am for whatever plans you have for me, but I have confidence in you and I like the agenda of your organization. So will join with you. I do make this reservation. I have very strong opinions on some matters that may differ from objectives of the organization and would like it understood that my differences be respected." Professor Williams extended his hand in congratulations on his acceptance and said, "Joseph, our organization is very strong on tolerance and any difference you have that doesn't violate our basic principles will be respected." He got to his feet and, wishing Joseph a "good day," said, "we shall meet again." As he left, Joseph sat and pondered this new development. He was pleased that the professor had given him recognition but felt challenged and overwhelmed by the possibilities it offered. Contemplating this new situation, he felt a strong desire to discuss it with Allison. What shaped this desire, he could not fathom. He liked her but was sure he did not love her. Something made him want to be closer to her. Some strange magnetic force urged him to confide in her. That he would gain strength and purpose just talking to her. Dedicated to his mission, he felt inadequate and incapable of meeting its high purpose. Talking to Allison might help clear the confusion disturbing him.

Deciding on action, Joseph got to his feet and went to the cafeteria. It was lunchtime, and he was sure that Allison would be sitting at her usual table with her friends. As he entered the cafeteria, he immediately spotted Allison. She was easy to recognize. She sat where the sunlight, striking her hair illuminating it in a golden glow that made her very noticeable. Joseph took a seat in an inconspicuous spot and waited until they were finished eating and started to leave. Joseph then walked and greeted Allson as she was leaving. She answered Joseph with a smile. He apologized for disturbing her and then said, "Allison, I would like to talk with you.. Would you meet me after class and go with me to the little coffee shop outside the main gate. We could have a snack and be able to talk. Allison considered it for a moment and then said, "I think I would like that," Joseph was delighted. "Great," he exclaimed, "Let's meet at six at the main entrance." Allison agreed and they parted.

Filled with anticipation, the rest of the time spent in class, passed very slowly. When the final class bell rang, Joseph hurried to his room and spent time making himself presentable for his date with Allison.At last the time came and he made his way to their meeting place. When he got there, Allison was not there but after a short anxious wait, she did appear looking cheerful and attractive. Without further delay, after greeting her warmly, Joseph took her arm and they left for the coffee shop.

They had about a ten-minute walk to reach the coffee shop, located just outside the main entrance to the University. During this time they engaged in pleasant small talk the weather was mild and pleasant and they enjoyed each other's company. When they entered the shop, they found it not too busy and were able to select a booth in a secluded corner..

After placing their order, they paused and looked at each other before Joseph spoke. "Allison," he said, "I have been wanting to talk with you. Earlier, I told you that I needed a confidant and felt you could be someone I could trust. I mentioned that I am carrying a heavy burden that troubles me. Something I am reluctant to discuss because it is so unreal that telling it could expose me to ridicule, humiliation and even questions as to my sanity. I have poised these same questions to myself. I hope you will not have that reaction but am relying on your honesty and understanding, not to solve my problem, but to simply listen without condemnation as I unburden myself to you. That will help dispel my feeling of loneliness, helplessness and isolation."

He was interrupted by the waitress bringing their orders. They both had ordered sandwiches and coffee and discontinued conversation while they ate. As she ate, Allison studied Joseph. She had been attracted to him from the first day they met. He was good looking on the edge of handsome but it was more than physical appearance that attracted her. There was an intensity within him that even when he was not doing anything seemed to exude from him. And when he looked at you it was as though his eyes penetrated through the outer shield of facial features into your very being. When he spoke his voice had a musical timbre that was unusual and ear catching. His approach conveyed a feeling of a warm, caring person. Altogether, she thought, a very interesting complex enigma and perhaps a dangerous one. She was getting involved with him and decided to be wary and on her guard. They finished eating and while sipping coffee, resumed their conversation. Allison said, "Frankly. Joseph, you have aroused my curiosity since I can't imagine what great burden a young, healthy, well-to-do, class A unencumbered male student could have that is not suited for experienced male ears but only suitable for those of a young unsophisticated woman. However, I am flattered by your choosing me and will hear you not as a critic but as a friend and confidant."

Joseph thanked her, and said, "Perhaps when you hear my experience you will understand my dillema." He then related the experience of his dream. The impelling force driving him to fulfill its demands. His interview with the school counselor and his parents. The frightening experience with the calling of his name out of the shrieking wind sounds. Now recently, Professor Williams calling on him to be a speaker at demonstrations seemed to be opening a window of opportunity to fulfill the message of his mission. His account had taken a good half hour and now he sat back and waited for Allison's reaction. She was silent for several minutes and then spoke carefully, "Joseph, do you believe you are a prophet?

Joseph thought and then answered. "I don't know, the idea scares me. I don't feel I have the strength or ability. Yet, I feel driven, out of control. Something is running me. I can't seem to change or stop it. Honestly, I am scared."

Allison asked another question, "Do you plan to change the world?"

Joseph laughed, "How can I change the world, I am a nothing?"

Allison asked again, "Joseph, would you like to change the world?"

Now Joseph's face turned grim and angry, "Yes," he exclaimed, "Yes, I do," and without thought, "Yes, I will." As these words exploded involuntarily from within him as though without his control he sank back a rage seething within him. Allison observed him with pained sadness permeating her features. Tears came to her eyes and she reached out and grasped Joseph's hand.

"Joseph," she said, "You are the Prophet." Her answer shocked Joseph. He leaned forward and searched her face. Within him there was a strange feeling of exultation. My God, he thought.she believes in me. The first and only one. I no longer am alone.

He had to have her answer so he asked, "Allison, you believe in me. You are the only one. What made you say that?"

She replied, "Joseph, There is something in you that is not of this world. I don't know what it is but I feel it strongly eminating from you. At the same time I feel great sadness and I don't understand that emotion. I do know that I believe in you and that destiny awaits you."

In silence, Joseph absorbed her reply. Her words helped fortify his belief in the validity of his mission. He felt an increase in confidence and purpose. Now, he needed to be alone to explore these new emotions and plan his future actions. He turned to Allison and said, "How can I ever thank you? Your support has lifted me from despair to one of purpose. Your belief in me may be misplaced but it encourages me to go on and test the goals I seek. And even if I fail and this entire enterprise proves a farce, I will still be grateful to you. For helping to give me the opportunity to try. When I chose you to be my confidant to whom I could bare my most intimate thoughts, I never dreamt what a fortunate choice I had made. You have exceeded all my expectations." Joseph rose and helping Allison to her feet, they left.

On the way home, holding hands in a warm clasp, they walked in silence. Each wrapped in the thoughts of their recent conversation. Arriving at the dormitory, they looked intently at each other. Joseph thanked her and expressed his desire to see her soon again. Allison nodded in agreement; they then said their goodbyes.

As he entered his dormitory room, Jack looked up from the book he was studying to greet him. "Well, stranger, it looks like you have a busy social agenda." Joseph smiled, "I suppose you will want to know the details?"

Jack responded, "No. That is an Eastern trait. Here in the West, we consider it an insult to pry into personal doings." Joseph said, "I approve of your Western culture, so my social doings will remain a deep dark secret."

"That's fine" Jack retorted, "but on a non-personal basis, don't you think you should hit the books for Professor Williams' O.K.corral showdown tomorrow?"

"Yes, in due time." Joseph replied. Removing clothing to make himself comfortable, he then sat and reviewed the events of his time with Allison and his new found resolves stirring within him.

Finally, heeding Jack's advice, Joseph took out a text and tried to study. But his mind refused to concentrate, the words he tried to read became blurred and meaningless. All his thoughts were filled with his conversation with Allison. He was puzzled by the way he exploded with the words, that he would change the world. And then by her declaration, through her tears, that he was the prophet, was inexplicable. Why the sadness? Why the tears? What would cause this unhappy emotion? He felt she was a remarkable person with unusual intuitive sensitivety. She believed he was the prophet with a mission to declare the truth. Did her feminine instincts alert her to the fate of those that dared to speak the truth? How the multitude would react with hate and violence against those that dare challenge the childish fantasies that men create to perpetuate their need for special privilege and power. Did she sense the final fate that awaits those who champion righteousness, justice, truth and peace? How many of these great icons have perished at the hands of the merchants of hate. Jesus, Lincoln, Ghandi, and many others, murdered, assassinated, killed. Did she believe that even the insignificant voice of mine could arouse a volume of hate and violence to silence me. I have no illusions that I could ever achieve a level of that importance. But I also understand that if one were to talk about removing the comfort blanket of immortality from the grasp of those who refuse to accept mortality a serious reaction could take place. There is a risk to speaking the truth, and what is true should be the aim of desirable discussion and not with those who feel they alone possess a privileged and restrictive truth. I hope to transverse this scene without fear. I know there all too many who preach love and practice hate. There is so much nobleness in man that needs to assert its self. I would like to be able to ignite that quality. The hour was getting late and Jack was readying for bed. Joseph decided to forego any further attempt to study and prepare for sleep. As he covered himself, he reached out to the universal energy and prayed, "Master of the Universe, give me strength, courage and wisdom."

CHAPTER 4

▼

The next morning, Joseph sat in Professor William's class. Professor Williams said, "We will begin our studies with the causes that led to the beginning of the American Revolution. European nations were battling for territory and commercial interests in the New World. In 1763, at the Treaty of Paris, Great Britain, France, Spain and Portugal ceded large portions of territory to their respective nations. Great Britain received Canada and most of the territory east of the Missippi. The seeds of the revolution were planted by England striving to rule the colonies by royal and parliamentary decrees without colonist participation. Taxes, boycotts, laws regulating imports and exports, all this without consultation or input from the colonials. At this time it is important to consider a factor that has received very little attention in most studies. That is the character of the colonials. They were a people bred in hardship, violence, a brutal environment and freedom from the cloistered confines of royal and state religion subservience. These elements produced a highly individualistic and independent people who considered themselves master of their fate and capable of meeting all challenges. It was failure to comprehend this new mold that led the Royal House to its mistaken policies that lost it its colonies and the great nation it was to become."

He ended his lecture and then assigned reading studies for their next session. As the students left, he motioned for Joseph to remain. After the classroom cleared, he addressed Joseph, "Joseph, a panel discussion has been scheduled for this coming Wednesday and our organization has been invited. We are asked to provide two participants and I would like you to attend. I have commitments that prevent my attendance. You will be joined by another of our members. The topic to be discussed is "Diversity" as it affects school and work. Can we count on you?" Joseph gave it some thought and then decided to agree, "Yes," he said, "Do you think I am qualified? Professor Williams smiled "I am sure you are, you will let me know how it went." He shook Joseph's hand and left.

Joseph made inquiries and learned that the panel discussion would take place under the auspices of the University and attended by representatives of interested groups, and by others considered experts in that field. The moderator would be an individual representing the University. Journalist and other media had also been invited. Attendance would be mostly students, however, advertised as of public interest, the public was invited. The size and scope of the event was intimidating to Joseph and his thoughts turned to Allison. He felt the need for reassurance he thought she could provide. At noon, he headed for the cafeteria, hoping he would be able to talk with her. She was sitting with friends and Joseph waited until they were leaving before approaching and seeking to detain her. She was happy to see Joseph and responded willingly to his request for a brief conversation. When seated at a table, He told Allison of the forthcoming panel meeting and his participation in it. Then looking directly at her, he said, "Frankly, I am very nervous about doing this. I needed to talk to you because somehow you make things clearer. You have the ability to quiet the disturbing thoughts rattling in my head. I know that I keep imposing on you, but what you say has become very important to me." Allison looked at him with a concerned expression, "Joseph, you don't impose, I am honored at the value you place on my words. I believe in you and in your mission.

Your only obstacle is your own self-doubt you refuse to accept the idea that you are gifted beyond the normal. Some undefined celestial authority has selected you because of your innate qualities for their or its purpose. I feel, you are involved with elements that cannot be described or understood." She reached across the table and taking his hand pressed it warmly. "Joseph," she said, "You must speak with power, authority and confidence. The words you speak will be your words but the message will be the one your voices defined, you are highly qualified for any discussion. Forget all your doubts and think only of purpose." They both were silent. Joseph studied her and thought. She is so beautiful, so good, so wise and intelligent. I think I adore her. Do I love her or is this really gratitude? As they got up to leave, Joseph kissed he hand and said, "Dear, dear confidant, thank you and God bless you." And then as an afterthought, "Will you attend? It will be comforting to have a friend there." Allison smiled, "Certainly, and I will bring my group with me."

The day of the meeting arrived and scheduled to begin at 6:30 P.M. It was held in the smaller assembly room with a seating capacity of 600. On the platform there were three microphone stands. The central one for the monitor, the other two for speakers. At the rear of the platform were six seats for the speakers. Joseph had arrived and joined the other participants gathered there. He engaged in conversation with the other member of their organization, whom he had met earlier. This individual was not a student, but a forty-year-old attorney with a successful practice in the city. They enjoyed a conversation until they were asked to take their seats as the meeting opened. The person conducting the meeting was a philosophy professor, middle age and with a commanding appearance and voice. He began by introducing himself. "I am Professor Walter Fields. We are meeting this evening to discuss Diversity and its effect on people and our country. This is our subject and I will define the rules for conduct of that discussion. Civility is required and personal, ethnic, or group disparagement will not be tolerated. The procedure to be followed will be threefold. First, those speaking in favor of Diversity; secondly those opposed to it, and third-questions from the audience. A traveling microphone will be available for floor questions. The individual selected shall give his name and status and permitted only to ask a question to whom he chooses for reply, but only the question, no statements or opinions, I will introduce each speaker, and they will say whom they represent. Your cooperation in observing our requirements will insure a productive and agreeable discussion, Thank you.

He then introduced the speaker, Mr. John Morgan who stepped up to the microphone and declared, "I represent an Afro-American organization that seeks to achieve its legitimate position in the economic, business, industry and political life of this nation. We see the concept of diversity as recognizing the reality that this nation made up of many different ethnic, religious, and cultural elements must accept the fact that the Anglo-Saxon control has been breached that minorities should have their day in the sun. As descendants of the victims of that great sin of slavery, we know many people of good will are striving to rectify that wrong and its consequences. But more needs to be done and changed. The current black population is about 14%. Justice should have that per-centage of blacks in corporations, politics, employment and juries. Diversity helps recognize minority cultures and traditions. Black history and culture, considered non-existing in the past, is now being exposed by the beneficial light of diversity. We want good things to happen." He closed and left to moderate applause.

Professor Fields then introduced the next speaker, Mr. Santos Ramirez. Mr. Ramirez spoke into the microphone. "I am Santos Ramirez and I represent a Latino organization that strives to retain our culture and traditions. We are grateful that we live in a country that recognizes diversity and respects our differences. We are good Americans and our contributions to this country are many. You have joined us in celebration of some of our holidays and allowed the Spanish language to enter common usage. You have welcomed us. We are a hard working, family devoted, and warm-hearted people. You have taken to our food, our music, and our life style that has added variety and color to the mosaic of this nation. There is concern about the influx of illegal immigrants. A sorrowful problem since it is human nature to escape privation for a better life. We hope for a humane solution." Saluting, he said, "Vaya con Dios," bowed, and left. The audience responded with applause.

When quiet was resumed, Professor Fields introduced the next speaker, "Thomas Clark,"is a well known author, lecturer and political activist." An elderly, well-dressed individual, Mr.Clark addressed the audience. "Students and fellow Americans, it is a privilege to speak to this cosmopolitan audience, of students and the general public. I represent an organization that strives for peace and global unity of all people. In the United States we recognize that all people are basically equal in qualities of intelligence, abilities and the striving for the blessings of peace and prosperity for themselves and familiy. Diversity justly recognizes that although we are all basically the same, we do have differences of religion, customs, tradition, and life style. These assume their rightful place in the scenario of our society. My organization feels that this formula of individual equality and group diversity is one that could successfully unite all people on earth into a unity of the human race that will diminish narrow national interests in favor of ideals that benefit all mankind. In that situation, national fervor that favors hostile activities would become impotent and allow the blessings of peace to fill the air. Critics will say, this leads to world government and the loss of sovereignty that enables a country to withstand foreign pressure that could harm its residents. That could be true if such arrangements were entered into precipitously without proper safeguards. Before such a move, a constitution would be needed to define the rights and protection of all participants. The future defines that human progress will require the establishment of a world authority that ends the bickering and hostilities of the many competing nations. For a unity that wll bring tranquility and peace to a world riven by hate, hostility, poverty and despair. My organization works and prays for that day." He sat down to rousing applause.

The next speaker was the other member of Joseph's organization. He was introduced as Paul Beck, a prominent attorney from the city. He spoke clearly and addressed his remarks to the topic Mr.Morgan had discussed. "Mr.Morgan," he said, "I agree whole-heartedly with your desire to see Blacks assume their rightful place in society. I also am aware of the discrimination that some practiced against your race and the shameful past of our history of that unforgivable sin of slavery your forebearers suffered. On some things, we differ. The rightful place in society should not be given by artificial quotas but should be earned by effort and self-discipline, unless you are gifted with an inheritence of wealth and prestige. Few of us are in that gilded position, and have achieved our social position, the old fashioned way. We worked hard and earned it. Mr.Morgan, the path to success for Blacks is difficult but not impossible. There are many obstacles to success not only outside but also inside your community. Discrimination is a factor but can be overcome since there is a large white population rooting for you. Permit me the presumption of offering a solution. First discard the identity of victim and the bugaboo of a white non-existing conspiracy to do you in. Admit the serious problems in your community of violence, drugs, fatherless mothers and work with local authorities to solve them. Encourage the talent, abilities and genius untapped in your people as demonstrated by many of your peers, who have contributed so much to our society. Mr.Morgan, we are with you." He stopped and acknowledged the heavy applause.

The next speaker introduced was a woman, identified as Susan Blake, an official of a City Social Service. She began by thanking the panel for inviting her to speak. She then addressed her remarks to the subject of Mr.Ramirez 's speech. "Mr.Ramiriz," she said, "You have made an excellent presentation of the positive and welcome influence of the Latino population. I have very little disagreement with what you have said. But as with most things, there is a negative side that needs attention and correction. Diversity is a desirable concept and its variety adds color and excitement to our lives. But in our social work, we are put in contact with distressing social problems caused by excessive influx of Latino illegal immigration. We even have a problem with legal Latino immigrants. This nation has always prided itself as a nation built by immigrants. But there is a major disturbing difference between past immigrants and current Latino immigrants. The steady flow of immigrants, mostly from Europe, to the United States consisted of those escaping poverty, religious and governmental oppression. They saw America as the sanctuary of freedom and superior in every way to what they had left behind. They had a fervent desire to become American citizens and strove to shed all aspects of their former foreign nationality, its customs, culture and language. Their descendents, completely assimilated could enter the educational system and work force indistinguable from those who had lived in America for generations. In the past several decades, we have witnessed an influx of immigrants who do not accept our culture or principles that created our prosperity and power. They maintain their own customs and language and even attempt to maintain their own legal systems. I consder this corruption of the concept of Diversity, a threat to the permanency and ideals of democracy. Those pouring across our open borders are seeking to escape poverty not to gain freedom. Arriving here, they are forced to work for wages insufficient to support a decent life style. Ten, twelve or more people living in a squalid two-bedroom unit is not uncommon. Schools, medical and social facilities are stretched beyond their financial limitations to provide needed care. These poor, impoverished people are victims of the greedy commercial and political interests on both sides of the border. Those responsible need to be called to account. Thank you." Long applause followed.

The next speaker called upon to speak was Joseph. He was introduced as a freshman student representing the student body and though a young freshman has a depth of knowledge and intellect worthy of being heard. On the news of a student speaker, the considerable student presence broke into tremendous applause and shouting of "hear, hear." Joseph acknowledged this ovation by raising his arms. When the tumult subsided, he spoke, "Thank you, fellow students for your warm welcome. I don't want to be misrepresented as speaking for all students since I am only expressing my own opinions which may be at variance with some or even a majority of the students," As he spoke, without the aid of a microphone the volume of his voice filled the auditorium and the musical quality of his words captured the rapt attention of his listeners. He opened with the question, "Is the current promotion and acceptace of diversity, good or bad for our nation? I believe, its emphasis is a threat to our nation. The original purpose of diversity was to give minoritys, self-esteem. They were not inferior but equal to any other culture. They had a history, culture and heritage that should make them proud and respected. This is the good side of the coin of diversity. There is a bad side to diversity that needs to be recognized and understood. Let us examine the meaning of the word, diversity. The dictionary defines it as the state of being different. We know and accept the differences that exist in all forms of existence and the differences among humans. This nation created a new unique government of melding all the diverse human elements into a common harmonius entity based on principles and laws that all could support. The motto"E Pluribus Unum", one out of many, exemplified the achievment of this unity and released the powers, existing in the people, for creativity and progress. The current attraction of diversity is promoting minority interests beyond thr limits of their justifiable requirements into political and other areas that impinge on the rights of others. As they gain political influence, they implement their own agenda that affects the nation's best interests. With "Many Out of One,"disunity will be complete.

To understand diversity and its effect on society, we must analyse the composition and behavior of the ethnic or racial minority groups involved in diversity. These groups are seperately composed of persons with their own individuality that distinguish them from each other.

But the group, as a whole, though composed of differing personalities, can and does display common characteristics and behavior patterns that could be classified as a stereotype. Here we run up against the prevalent requirement of political correctness. Which forbids statements that any group has faults and may not be equal to the best in our society. But groups, like individuals, have characteristics and behavior resulting from centuries of environmental, and heritage development. They may have customs, culture, and religious practices that are in conflict with laws and requirements of the host society. Intelligent discussion that seeks to solve serious problems requires respect for differing views, but must operate on a basis that all ideas are open for discussion and that nothing is sacred and immune from questioning. While a just society rules that all are equal under the law, it should also be accepted that not all are equal physically, mentally or in behavior. Equality supporters claim women should be considered equal to men in sports, military and occupations where heavy physical requirements have led to the stronger male dominance. Logic and common sense that disputes this is repudiated. The basic legal and humane rights of women are a proper equality rights concern. There is one element that exists throughout the universe. It is possesed by every microscopic chemical or organic entity as well as the highest and lowest forms of life. That is the force for survival. It is manifested in everything, as it is in man, who sought through the family, the tribe, the people, the nation for survival. Survival of the species is a basic law of nature. The struggle for minority groups to establish their rightful position is a struggle for survival and should be appreciated as such but it should not be used to give them excess power for an agenda harmful to the nation's unity. The false doctrine that everyone is the same should be eliminated and replaced with the truth. Thank you." He bowed and left to a standing ovation.

Professor Fields assumed the microphone and said,"Joseph, I compliment you on your excellent presentation. You have justified your appearance and your representation of our students is an erudite example of the quality of our students." His statement was greeted by loud applause. Professor Fields smiled and when the applause subsided, spoke. We will now take questions from the floor. Please, raise your hand and if recognized state your name and position and direct your question at the panelist, whose answer you seek." He pointed and a student stood up and declared, "I am a senior student and my question is directed to Mr.Morgan. Do you think it is fair for Affirmative Action to insure preference for an individual who has a much lower score and academic performance than a student with a very high score, who is denied admission in favor of the lower score applicant?" Mr.Morgan replied, "All things being equal, that wouldn't be fair. But unfortunately, things aren't equal. The recipient of that preference is the product of a slave dynasty that impaired normal progress in economics, education, and social development. That person also has to contend with racial discrimination that makes obtaining employment, good education and other benefits of our society a struggle. A level playing field requires some adjustments to reduce unjustified obstacles raised by a white power structure striving to maintain control. When true equality is finally achieved, corrective measures will no longer be needed or desired." Professor Fields then designated another student. He stated, he was Tom Warren a third-year student and addressed Mr.Ramirez with his question. "I am fond of Latinos but question their failure to accept our principles and resist assimilation. Many of us whose parents were innigrants spoke to us in their native tongue and we replied in English. They tried their best to speak English. Our experience with Latino workers, who have been in this country for years, still do not speak or understand English. Their decendents, born in this country, will converse with each other in Spanish. Politicians catering to the Latino vote have augmented this tendency by promoting the use of Spanish in public and business facilities. A common language binds a nation together. Accepting a second language, as in Canada, can cause a breech from the main body of the nation. Why this refusal to accept our language and culture?" Mr.Ramirez thought awhile before answering. "I am going to be honest and say, I don't know. I will give my opinion on some factors that may be the reason but don't know if they are correct. First, there is such warm reception to all things spanish, the food, the music, the culture, the language, the people, so there is little pressure to change to a culture that perhaps has less warmth. Secondly, they really love being the way they are and are satsfied in it since they can function comfortably within its boundaries. There is assimilation with many later generations who have realized that to attain economic, political and social progress they must adopt the "American mode" and have proven they can achieve these goals. This may not answer your question but is the best answer my limited comprehension can provide. Tom Warren thanked him and led the heavy applause.

Professor Fields recognized another individual. This person was not a student. He spoke, "I am Philip Ross, a journalist from our local city paper and I have a question for Mr.Clark. I want to first express my deep respect for his many fine written works, his unselfish devotion to many worthy causes and that any criticism I may voice is abstract and not directed at him. If you will permit familiarity, Tom, you seek to promote a world government based on individual equality and group diversity. This formula, in my opinion does not lead to unity but to disunity. Historically, world governments have not succeeded because of these elements. The League of Nations was a dismal failure. The current United Nations is impotent. Its membership of 191 nations is overwhelmingly run by dictators. They usually vote for donations or measures against their fancied enemies. How can this be overcome?" Mr. Clark responded, "Thank you, Phil, for your kind compliments and I assure you that in discussions that search for truth all opinions are welcomed and respected, I agree that past efforts to establish a world body that enforces peace and the well being of all people has been unsuccessful. Objectives for a world body that serves the best interests of all nations cannot be built on the nations present objectives. A majority of nations are cursed with corrupt and demagogic governments engaged in hate and violence. Effecting change will take years of pressure, education, diplomacy and assistance. The cure will be the transforming of these from dictator ruled nations to democracy and people rule. Then you will have moral and law observing nations capable of supporting the moral and lawful duties of a world body. My organization believes this will happen in the future and we urge all to join in making this vision an eventual reality." He finished and held up his arm in salute to the resounding applause.

Professor Fields stepped up to the microphone and declared, "Time will not permit additional questions and dictates closing this meeting. I would like to add my compliments to all participating. The panel members and the members of the audience for their excellent presentations and questions. In the past, some meetings have been disturbed by loud and disrupting demonstrators seeking to enforce their views by violence. This meeting was a model of intelligent, thoughtful and meaningful discussion and all have earned our heartfelt thanks and gratitude. I now declare the meeting closed. Thank you." Instant and long applause followed. Before leaving, the panel members shook hands and exchanged pleasantries. Joseph spoke briefly to the other member of his group and then descended from the podium to search for Allison.

Allison and her friends had remained behind, as the audience left, so Joseph had no difficulty in locating them. He was greeted warmly and they all complimented him on his presentation. He offered to take all four to the cafeteria for refreshments but, except for Allison, declined. They left and Joseph was alone with Allison. She had accepted his offer and Joseph delighted, took her arm and they left. He was anxious to talk with her but she said to wait until they were seated and comfortable. Arriving at the cafeteria they selected a table and Joseph left to obtain the items desired. When seated with their refreshments, Joseph looked at Allison waiting for her remarks. After a pause, she said, "Joseph, I am proud of you. You came across with such power, clarity, and depth of intellect that everyone was captivated. You had their complete attention throughout your talk. You spoke with confidence and authority. Evidently you have the power to hold an audience with your words. You are a gifted orator." Joseph shook his head, "Allison, you are creating an image of me that I am having difficulty in believing. You see things in me that are not visible to me. You say my words have power but look at the power your words have on me and how they guide and motivate me. Your words have given me the confidence and purpose I express. Your loyalty and concern quiets the turmoil within me and helps me keep my balance. I am so grateful to you." Allison said, "I believe in you, but more important, you must believe in yourself. The qualities I see in you are not figments of my imagination but very real and perhaps disturbing, I know in time, you will recognize them as an ingredient of your mission, a mission ordained by we know not what. As to your gratitude it is accepted as an appetizer," Joseph was silent. He studied her long and hard, looking into her eyes. Unflinching, she returned his gaze. Finally said, "Allison, you have become very dear to me. I have questioned if my feelings were love or gratitude. To me, declaring love for a future mate is a momentous decision. Not to be taken lightly since it is a lifelong commitment. I have thought a lot about it and hesitate. I'm still not sure. Allison lowered her eyes and then looking at him directly spoke. "Joseph, I also know that declaring one's love is a momentous decision. But I am sure," then softly, "I love you, with all my heart and soul. I love you," Joseph sat back, dumbfounded. He looked at her as emotions raged through his body. This beautiful, wonderful woman had expressed love for him. This unbelievable, incredible event was actually happening to him. He reached over and taking her hands in his, pressed them warmly. Emotions locked within his breast suddenly burst their bonds and leaped in words from his mouth. "Allison, I do love you, I adore you. I really didn't believe you could love me. I promise to dedicate the rest of my life to your happiness," Allison smiled "No, Joseph your dedication must be to the requirements of your mission. I know that is something you cannot deviate from.or set aside. I will be satisfied with the warmth of knowing you love me and I will try to be your helpmate. Your doubts about your love for me was never a question in my mind. Your every word, gesture, action gave me all the truth I needed to tell me of your love. I really didn't need your words but expressing them has made me supremely happy." Joseph grinned. "You amaze me. Where did you obtain your wisdom? Elderly sages who have spent a lifetime pursuing knowledge, do not display your wisdom. I suppose you were born with it. It's getting late, and I better release you. This day's happenings has changed my life and filled it with joy. I see nothing but blue skies smiling above. As they got up and prepared to leave, Allison smiled, "From the song of the same name? I have a request and I know this is a public place but I feel it appropiate to offer you my lips to seal our love." Joseph was in ecstasy, "Allison your words have taken me to the gates of heaven and now you let me enter with your kiss." Embracing her, they kissed. They left and went towards her dormitory. Joseph was exhilarated. He felt he was walking on air. He held her arm closely. The warmth of their love was like a physical presence enveloping them. They walked in silence wrapped in their emotions that like a magnetic current bonded them together. They continued in silence until they reached her dormitory. He took her aside to a secluded area and then hugging her tightly, kissed her passionately and looking deeply into her eyes, said "I love you, I love you," Tears were in her eyes, as Allison responded, "Thank you, I love you too." Taking her to the entrance and bidding her farewell, Joseph left to walk to his dormitory. His mind was racing with the unbelievable events of the day. A tremendous change in his life had happened. New vistas had opened, new horizons that needed comprehension and perhaps new planning for the future. The idea of a permanent life with Allison as his wife was a delight beyond any past imagining. How wonderful that would be. But, what about his mission? Do I discard that in favor of domestic bliss? What about our difference in religious beliefs, is that a serious obstacle? My mission can I forget it and will that cause the unbearable loss of Allison if I persist? These are problems I must think through. All

I am certain of is that I love Allison more than life. I don't want to lose her. I need time, I need help. Arriving at his residence door he ended his mental search for answers. On his entry into his room, he was greeted by Jack, deep in his studies. Divesting himself of some clothing, Joseph picked up a book and began studying.

CHAPTER 5

▼

The next morning they entered Professor Williams's class. On entry, Joseph was greeted by Professor Williams, who shook his hand and said, "I want to congratulate you on your fine presentation at the panel discussion. I spoke to our other member panelist, Paul Beck, who was very impressed with your delivery, and gave me a detailed account of its program and of your outstanding performance. You have over justified my confidence in you. We all thank you." Joseph thanked him for his kind words. Professor Williams continued, "Joseph something has come up that may cause you problems. I want to discuss it with you, so if you could meet me in my office after my classes, I will want to talk with you." Joseph frowned, "Can you tell me what it is?" Professor Williams shook his head, "No, it could be rather lengthy which my time will not allow. If you will meet me in my office before lunch, I will be able to give a full explanation." In puzzlement, Joseph agreed. As he sat in class, Joseph worried about Professor Williams remark that there was something that could cause him problems. He hoped it had nothing to do with his relations with Allison. Perhaps someone had witnessed his hugging and kissing her. Could that be a violation of some university rule? Well, he thought, the professor would explain. He knew the professor liked him and felt he would do his best to protect him. Consoled by these thought, he put aside his worries and decided to be patient and keep his appointment with Professor Williams.

At the designated time, Joseph reported to Professor Williams's office. The door was open and the professor was seated at his desk. The professor called to him to enter, asked him to shut the door and take a seat close by him. After Joseph was seated there was a moment of silence, while the Professor studied him. He then spoke, "Joseph what I am about to tell you may prove out to be nothing but my experience has taught me to prepare for any feasible eventuality. I feel obligated to make you aware of a situation that could affect you. This is what has happened. Before entering this university, you told your parents that you had received a celestial message that you were a prophet, and were prepared to shelve everything to pursue that objective. They induced you to continue your education but being concerned as to your mental state, they consulted a psychiatrist. He, on his own, decided to check with us as to your progress and behavior. I was called in as were your other instructors for a report on your scholastic performance and attitude. Those of us, who worked with you, gave you an excellent rating in every category. The Dean then did something stupid. At the usual faculty meeting, attended by all the faculty, he related the psychiatrist request and the reason motivating that request. He worded the reason as based on your claim to being a prophet, designated by heavenly powers. I objected and countered that knowing you, was certain you made no such claim and that such interpretation had no validity. The Dean admitted he had no solid information on the accuracy of that story, and asked the faculty to disregard it. He told the faculty that divulging what they had heard could have serious repercussions, and asked them to take a solemn oath not to divulge to anyone what they had heard and they all agreed. That, normally, should end it except my knowledge and experience with human nature knows that any juicy tidbit of gossip develops a life of its own and soon, regardless of secrecy requirements will rise and become public. I fully expect this tale to soon be known to the students, who may use it to badger and humiliate you. I want you to prepare yourself as to how you will respond to this if it occurs." Joseph was shocked and deeply troubled by this revelation. Deeply disturbed, he uttered, "I can't understand my parents doing this." Professor Williams answered." Don't be too hard on them. They did this because of their love and concern for you. When you are a parent you will understand the intricacies of parental love. But for now, let us concentrate on immediate issues. In order for me to help you in this matter, I need to know the actual basis for this prophet talk. Would you like to tell me?"

Joseph did not hesitate, "Professor Williams, I feel you are not only my mentor but a true friend. I trust you completely. Here is what happened. It may not make sense to you as it has not to others and at times even not to me, but it rules me and so dominates me that I am left with no choice. I don't believe in heavenly powers that concerns itself with the human race. But something is going on that I can't understand." Joseph then related his dream. Its impact, his consultations with counselor and parents their disparagement and finally that Allison, whom he loved, was the only one who supported his vision. He finished and looked at the Professor. The Professor had been listening intently as Joseph finished, he pursed his lips and lowered his head in thought. There was an extended period of silence. He finally raised his head and looking at Joseph said, "You have told me of an incredible event and the very strong effect it had on you. I am a realist and my initial reaction would be to join the naysayers, discount your dream and advise you to ignore it. But being a true realist requires me to admit there are things in the universe beyond our comprehension or ability to understand. This force that drives you is real, the effect it has on you is real, despite your efforts to deny it. I know now that you never claimed to be a prophet. That you had miraculous powers that you spoke with and were spoken to by God. You claim none of these things, but are in a struggle with a force demanding you deliver a message of truth to a world that denies and perverts the truth. You do not feel equal to that task, but feel forced to continue. I don't know where this will lead but

I respect you and your humility and sincerity. As much as I can, I will defend and support you. The world badly needs a spokesman for the truth to destroy the superstition and evil that is dooming our planet. Perhaps, you are that one. I would be overjoyed if you are. If that comes about and you are the one, I will kneel and pay you homage." He got to his feet, walked to Joseph and extended his hand. Joseph was stricken speachless. This endorsement from a highly educated and intelligent professor was overwhelming and that he had earned a friend in exalted position was elating. He grasped the extended had with both of his and expressed his heartfelt thanks for this most unexpected and encouraging talk. Leaving the office, Joseph felt the need to see Allison and tell her of these latest developments. He rushed to the cafeteria, knowing it was late and hoping she was still there. As he arrived, he saw Mallory and another friend still seated there. He went to them and asked for Allison, Mallory pointed to the exit and said, "She just left," Joseph rushed out of the exit door and saw Allison walking. He called to her, she heard him and turned and waited. Reaching her, he asked if she had time to talk. Receiving her agreement, he led her to a seat in a shaded area. After some initial pleasantries, Joseph spoke about his meeting with Professor Williams and the problem created by the Dean's comments at the faculty meeting. "Allison," Joseph said, "Professor Williams said the students would soon know about it and will start badgering me. He warned me to be prepared and think about how to respond. My initial reaction would be to denounce them and be prepared for the use of a physical reply. How does my wise and beautiful sweetheart think I should reply?" Allison thought and thanking him for the compliment said, "Darling, that approach is wrong and will only cause you more serious trouble. You can turn these things into harmless entities with humor. Such as, I really meant p-r-o-f-i-t or look in your newspaper for the next announcement. Humor can trivialize the most important issues. That confounds people looking for a strong reaction." Joseph smiled, "Your wisdom amazes me. I will act just as you say. You are such a wonderful help to me. I couldn't do without you. You are the rock, I plan to build my life on." Allison smiled, "I hope to be more comfortable than a rock." Joseph laughed, "I am most certain you will be. There is more to tell. Professor Williams said he needed to know what really happend so he could properly defend me. Feeling that I could trust him, I told him everything, I even told him that I loved you and that you were the only one that believed in me. He then went through it all with me and said that even though he was skeptical, he still recognized there were things beyond our comprehension and certain things about my experience impressed him. He ended up by saying that he could accept the possibility of me as the messenger and that he would defend and support me and if it turned out I was, he would pay me homage. I now have a real friend in high places. Allison was delighted at this turn of events, she told him. "Everything that is happening is as though some giant hand is turning the wheel of your destiny towards a determined goal. I feel you have the ability for real greatness and hope and pray that your destiny permits me a place in your life and love." Joseph's face saddened, "Allison without your love and presence my life would be empty and barren. Drab, grey, merciless and undesirable. You are the light of my life and love. I couldn't live without you, I want to marry you." Allison took his hand, "And I want to be your wife, friend and your helper in any endeavour you choose. But we must wait until we are older and complete our education. Then we will be ready for the responsibilities of adults. For a home and the treasure of children." Joseph nodded his agreement and then entered a new subject, "Allison, I want no obstacle to our future hope of marriage so would like clarification of our religious beliefs that would affect our children. You were raised Protestant and I am Jewish. I deviate from my religion in the sense that I do not accept the concept of a God who is personally involved or has a plan for the human race. I do accept the moral teachings and the laws derived from ages of experience that we are required by law to obey. There is no doctrine on heaven or hell and life must be lived now and not in preparation for death and an unproven immortality. And finally, that life is determined by deeds not faith. I can accept these precepts. Your religion teaches that a human being was a God and is so worshiped. That faith takes precedence over deeds. I would have difficulty accepting these premises. Tell me your thoughts and I will respect them." Allison thought and then remarked, "Although I was raised a Protestant, my parents were more concerned with the moral message of the faith rather than the ritualistic symbolism. As I grew older, I had serious doubts about the credibility of a heaven or hell. The concept of immortality was also troubling because I don't know what I could be doing for a million or more years, since, perhaps, ninety percent of our pleasure in life eminates from the physical I will say as Ruth in the Bible said, 'Whither thou goest, I will go. Whither thou lodgest, I will lodge. Your faith will be my faith.'" Joseph leaned over and kissed her and said, "My dearest wife to be. I adore you." They chatted for a while then Allison said, "It's time for class." They got up and after an affectionate embrace, left for their respective classes."

CHAPTER 6

▼

The next two weeks were filled with activity scholastic and social. Joseph and Allison spent as much time together as they could arrange. Their relationship had blossomed into a very close bonding of mutual interests and physical attraction. They cared for each other with a deep and abiding love that manifested itself with the utmost sensitivity to each other. They were so in love with each other and enjoyed the atmosphere of activity and tranquility that surrounded them. Then one day, their quiet was shattered by a voice. That voice directed at Joseph, harshly yelled. "Hey prophet Joseph, how about a good tip on the stock market." Joseph strolling with Allison, was startled.his body trembled as a flood of rage suffused it and his face grew angry and red. With fists clenched he was about to respond with fury, when he felt Allisons hand tugging at him. He recollected himself, paused and then with a laugh shouted, "Sure, buy low, sell high." The voice was silent Allison was grateful and complimented him on controlling himself and responding corretly. Joseph said, "I think I'm getting smarter. I listen to you. Professor Williams was right the news is out and I can expect a lot of this. I wonder where the one who yelled at me got his information." Allison said, "Just handle it as you just did and it will go away. Don't lose your composure. I want you to promise that." Joseph hugged her, "Yes, counselor, I know better than to dispute your wisdom." Hand in hand, they continued their stroll.

The next few weeks were misery for Joseph. Word that he considered himself a prophet and could predict future events was widespread throughout the university and even reached the public in the city. An article in the university paper, although not identifying the student, ran the story about a freshman student, who claimed to be a prophet, who spoke with God. Although unidentified, it was common accepted knowledge that it was Joseph. Joseph had taken a disclaimer to the editorial office, but it was not printed or acknowledged. In accordance with his promise to Allison, Joseph suppressed his normal angry retorts and replied with humor. Although it did seem to turn aside more violent behavior, not being able to vent his anger was frustrating. He decided to talk with Professor Williams and get his advice. He approached Professor Williams after the morning class and apprised him of the situation and his correctness in predicting it. He also told the Professor of the first incidence and how he had heeded Allison's advice and answered it with humor. He then asked for the Professor's advice. The Professor said, "I congratulate you on your choice of a very savvy young lady. Her advice to you is perfect. It is better than the advice I would have given, which would be to ignore it. Her advice is much better and deprives the assailant of the power to respond or provoke. Stay the course she has set for you and you will outlast it." Joseph thanked him, they shook hands and parted.

PART II

CHAPTER 1

▼

During the following weeks, the harassment of Joseph on campus had lessened somewhat. Joseph had become quite creative in developing humerous responses to the badgering language hurled at him. Heeding Allison's advice had proven quite effective in diminishing the initial hostility and changed it into a friendly student ribbing. This was not the case in the public's response to this event. The news of Joseph's suppose claim of heavenly powers had been published in the local newspaper and picked up and promulgated nationally by the news media. The result was a flood of mail, addressed to Joseph. Some of the letters expressed belief that he was the Messiah, mentioned in the scriptures, come to straighten out the world's problems. Some tried to convert him so that he could bring his heavenly powers to their church. The majority of the letters were angry and reviled him as a false prophet seeking to discredit their religion for publicity and financial gain. Joseph was distressed by this unwarranted publicity and its undesired reaction. He, after consultation with Allison and Professor Williams, decided to ignore and not answer any of the mail. Instead, he would concentrate on removing himself from the limelight. This was becoming increasing difficult because of his increasing notoriety. To achieve obscurity, Joseph restricted his movements to his classes, his room, study hall, the library, and secluded meetings with Allison.

He refused interviews by the school publication and city journalist. He would only enter discussions with Professor Williams, Allison and his room mate Jack.J ack was puzzled by all the furor and couldn't understand what was going on. What he did understand was that Joseph, whom he liked and considered a friend, was under attack. He asserted his friendship to Joseph and told him, he would stand by him against all opposition. Joseph expressed his gratitude with thanks, and then clasping Jack in a hug, said, "You are a true friend." Joseph spent considerable time in meditation. He felt like a sailor in a storm at sea, tossed about by events over which he had no control, with eyes fixed on a guiding star. His star was Allison, Professor Williams and Jack. They gave him a sense of stability when events seemed to destroy the foundation on which he stood. He was having trouble concentrating on his studies. Much as he tried to isolate himself from the stresses of his situation it still intruded and affected his mental composure. His greatest solace and comfort was Allison's constant emphasis on confidence in his self, and that patience was required for a situation that was only temporary. They met frequently and the harmony of their thoughts and actions intensified the depths of their love.

The scene now shifts to a palatial suite office in a high-rise office building in New York City. An emergency board meeting of the national television station EGR is convened. Fourteen board members are present, and seated at the head chair is the president of the company, Alvin Tucker. He is in his middle seventies, white hair, a bit overweight, and wearing a grim expression. The meeting is called to order and Tucker speaks. "I called this emergency meeting because our ratings are heading towards the basement. In the last three months are ratings have dropped ten points. The reason is obvious, our programs stink. Those of you responsible for programing have evidently lost touch with the public, and have produced programs that no one cares to watch. This is very serious, I don't intend to see the demise of this company, so I am telling you things have to change. I am not saying heads will roll, but I am saying they must improve. Now, I am going to open this meeting for meaningful discussion and corrective action. The first speaker is Sid Foster, our vice-president in charge of programing." Foster spoke from his seat. "Determing what the public wants is difficult. The entire gamut of sports, crime, religion, sex, game shows, politics, comics, news, entertainment, and situationals is a vast field that frequently changes. One of the most durable appeals seems to be sex. The Steward Hern program that deals in outrageous sexual antics is extremely popular with a huge devoted following. That is a field we are wisely forbidden. Game shows that pay huge monetary prizes are very popular and our attempts failed because we could not compete with the popular "Feel the Fortune" and "Liability." Our situational comic program also failed expectations. We will need some time to review, analyse and study the current market and have a general overhaul of our approach." Tucker nodded his head, "I agree. Let's have more discussion. I want anyone with ideas to speak up. No matter what they are. Even an outlandish idea may have something valuable in it. So speak up." One of the members raised his hand. Tucker said, "O.K., Bill." Bill said, "It seems the public responds to stories of individuals unique experiences. There is a story of a Mexican peasant who found an image of the Virgin Mary on a cloak of his and a thousand or more people have traveled to his residence to see it. I wondered if we brought him in for a public interview on our station if that might be of important interest." This item was debated at some length until Tucker turned to the program director, Foster, for his comment. Foster said, I agree that individual unique experience is of interest to the general public, but I think acting on a statement of a Mexican peasant with something that could be proven illusionary would be extremely risky." Tucker said, "I agree. I see Tom Phelps has raised his hand. Go ahead Tom." Tom spoke, "I was thinking of this, but didn't think it worth mentioning until Bill brought up his thought and I saw it got serious consideration. So here is one that may be of interest. This story has been printed in several national newspapers and aroused considerable reaction. It concerns a young freshman student at Slocum University, who is said to consider himself ordained by God and who claims to speak to God. He has aroused a storm of reaction of people who support him and say he is the new messiah and others, a majority, who feel he is a con man seeking publicity and profit. Perhaps interviewing him on national television could be a winner for us." These comments caused a period of silence, while each member gave it their serious consideration. Finally Foster spoke, "Tom, my initial reaction to your presentation is positive. This has many of the ingredients of public appeal. Religion, which is always a hot topic. It is national and local and involves a university student, always always good because anything about universitys is of publics concern. That some consider he could be the messiah has earth shaking potential. Quite frankly, I like it and want Alvin"s opinion." Mr.Tucker did not hesitate, "I think this could become a very hot nationally and even internationally." Getting to his feet he turned to Foster and said, "The ball is in your court. I say go with it and keep me advised of your plans effecting this." They shook hands and he left. After he was gone, Mr.Foster took charge of the meeting and said, "I will pick the team to work with me on arranging the interview with this budding messiah. Tom this is your idea so you will be my second in command. I want Bill, Sheila, Corinne, and Mia. The rest of you are excused. When they left, Foster addressed his team. This is a big project whose success can insure our job security.Mr.Tucker very clearly implied that unless we moved forward, heads would roll. He wasn't joking. This may be an opportunity to save the company. That may require all our skill, experience and knowledge. So here is a plan on how we can proceed. The first step is to learn everything we can about him. His family background, His likes and dislikes. Does he have any bad habits, addictions, drugs, alcohol? Does he have obsessions, and what are they? What about women, does he pursue them, sex, pornography, does he have a steady girl friend? What subjects does he take and is he a good student? These are things we must know. Sheila and Mia, I am assigning you the task of acquiring that intelligence for us. Our next step is to get his agreement to appear for the interview. In many cases, the idea of being able to appear on national television and national exposure will cause a ready acceptance. In some cases, the offer is rejected, for different reasons, some worthy and some unworthy. Bill you will have the job of obtaining his agreement to appear. You will be assisted by Corinne. Your initial approach should be to present the benefits of appearing on national television. All expenses of travel, food, accommodations at the best hotel, and recreational expenses incurred during his stay will be paid by our firm. In the event that doesn't work, we are prepared to offer a substantial payment for his appearance. Depending on the intelligence disclosed, we can exploit any weakness he displays by providing complete satisfaction for any such special need. This roughly defines the procedure, the area and the financial resources available. I am available at all times for assisting you in any way I can, the time to begin this effort is now. Check with my staff tomorrow morning to receive papers and funds for your venture. He then shook each one's hands and wishing them good luck and success, left. The others remained and began a serious discussion on how to shape their plans.

The next morning, they went to Foster's office and picked up papers, travel tickets, funds, and since Slocum University was located in California. left for the airport. The flight was uneventful and arriving at their destination, went to their hotel. They spent the rest of the day getting settled. Tom Phelps was in charge of the team and working with Bill Halpern and Corinne Freeman made a call to the Slocum Dean's office to arrange an appointment with Joseph. After a considerable wait, Tom received a return call from the Dean's office that the request for an appointment with Joseph had been rejected by Joseph. A second call was made to the Dean's office and Tom spoke and emphasized the importance and prestige of his company and demanded to know the reason for refusal to meet with a representative that could benefit him. The Dean's secretary replied that Joseph had given explicit instructions, he was opposed to any publicity, interviews with media or anything that disturbed his privacy including conversations with supposed benefactors. Tom argued the point with her but was told, Joseph would not budge and further disputation was useless. This news left the team in a quandary. How to proceed? They debated this fiercely. Finally, Tom said, "Our only chance is a personal confrontation. We will have to sneak into the university and catch him alone, so we can talk to him. Since a woman can more easily move about, we will use Corinne to try to corner him and Bill and I will then move in. We must have the opportunity to talk and persuade him. They all agreed to this action. Tom then turned to Corinne, "You will have to spend some time learning his schedule. His classes, his lunch period, and where he spends his free time and how. That will help us decided the best time and place to confront him. Bill, you look young enough to be taken for a student. Mingle with them and pick up information, you can about him. Sheila and Mia, I know you are gathering intelligence. Do your best to speed it up that may become crucial. It looks like a bumpy road that we will have to overcome, but we can't give up. "They all signified their agreement.

CHAPTER 2

▼

After a two-week wait, Tom called a meeting to determine the results of their efforts and their next course of action. He asked Sheila and Mia for their intelligence report on Joseph. Sheila spoke, "We have done a complete research on him with the following findings. He is an individual with superior intelligence that he demonstrates with top grades in all his studies. Coming from a well-to-do family of devoted parents, has no financial problems or family difficulties. He has a shy nature that avoids prominence but speaks out forcefully about his beliefs. We discovered no discernible bad habits or obsessions. He does have one obsession, if you can call it that, is his love for his girfriend, Allison. The other obsession he claims, is a love for the truth. He is very selective of his friends, has few close friends, to whom he is very devoted. He is fond of discussion of important subjects and has humility and openness towards differing opinions. He has no regard for success measured in dollars and is above monetary appeal. He believes he has a mission to declare the truth. His high moral character is going to make him a tough nut to crack." Sheila finished, and she and Mia were thanked by Tom for an excellent comprehensive report. Tom then turned to Bill with a question, "Bill, what did you learn from the other students?" Bill responded, "Everything I learned, verifies Sheila and Mia's findings. The article in the school paper labeled him a prophet, which he never claimed. And the initial reaction was disparagement and ridicule, but Joseph's good humor response and unobtrusive behavior earned him respect and tolerance. They now regard him as their own deserving respect and acceptance. Since all this furor broke, Joseph has pretty much isolated himself and tries to avoid unnecessary public exposure. He engages only in perfunctory conversation with the other students, and only speaks freely with his professors, Allison and her friends and his roommate Jack. While the students may engage in friendly taunting of Joseph, they would fly to his defense against outsiders. They consider Joseph, their prophet and have real affection for him. We must be extremely careful not to do anything that could be interpreted as harmful to Joseph as that would bring the entire student body with wrath down on us." Bill finished and was thanked by Tom. Tom then addressed the team. "These reports have made it abundantly clear that the appeal of money won't work, that appealing to ego for a national appearance won't work. That student pressure on him, won't work. That exploiting some weakness or obsession won't work since he doesn't seem to have any. So we will proceed with our original plan which will be to achieve a personal contact with him so we can persuade him. Corinne, were you able to work out a schedule of his activity and locations where he would be vulnerable to our confrontation?" Corinne answered, "Yes, I have prepared a detailed schedule, time, place, and location where he will be and those areas most suitable underlined in red." She walked over to Tom and handed him the paper. Tom thanked her and said, "We will get together tomorrow after I have studied this schedule and then determine our course of action," He then thanked and dismissed the team.

The next day, Tom met with Bill and Corinne to discuss the best site to achieve contact with Joseph. Corinne said the best opportunity would be the cafeteria where Joseph would be having lunch with Allison. They invariably stayed on, chatting, when most others had left. Tom disagreed. He wanted to meet Joseph alone and felt Allison presence would be detrimental. Corinne argued it would be difficult to catch him alone, since he spent all his free time with her. The only time he was alone was when leaving her, he headed for his room. Attempts to delay him then would be sure to fail. Tom gave this statement a great deal of thought and then said, "I don't like the idea of Allison's presence. We know she has a great deal of influence on him She is an unknown quantity that could upset our best efforts. Corinne has the best insight to this puzzle, so if you all agree, we will go ahead with the plan of a cafeteria confrontation." He called for a show of hands, and they all agreed. They then discussed the arrangements for that meeting. Corinne had suggested Friday's lunch period as the most suitable time, which was accepted. The plan developed was for two women, Corinne and Mia to occupy an adjoining table and engage in brief conversation with Joseph and Allison. Tom and Bill would join them a bit later for coffee. After most of the patrons had left leaving them somewhat isolated, Tom would make his approach, first with introducing themselves and then launching into his persuasive effort to induce Joseph's agreement to an interview.

Friday's lunch period arrived and the agreed on plan was put into effect. Corinne and Mia occupied a table close to the table occupied by Joseph and Allison. Mia greeted them and introduced herself and Corinne to them. They responded graciously and resumed their intense conversation. More and more of the students, who had been dining, left and soon the cafeteria with the exception of the two occupied tables was almost empty. At that time, Tom and Bill made their appearance and after introducing themselves to Joseph and Allison, joined Corinne and Mia with coffee. They were all engaged in conversation/but then as Joseph was preparing to get up and leave, Tom arose and went over to him. He said, "Mr.Stern, I don't want to approach you under false premise. I am not a student and have come here with a specific purpose, which I am now prepared to disclose to you. You, whether you acknowledge it or not, have become a person of national interesr. The public wants to know more about you and if you have a message for them from a heavenly source. There deep concern cannot be ignored and place s a responsibility on you to respond. You have indicated a desire to avoid all publicity and seek to secure your privacy, this is understood and most commendable. However, there are times when the public's interests overrides personal desires, no matter how worthy. I believe, this is such a time. That being true, what is the best means for your response? It should be made in a highly regarded and respected media that will protect the integrity of your remarks. I represent an organization that can provide that. My company the EGR national television station is one of the nation's largest. We can provide you with the platform to define yourself to a world anxious to hear from you. You can be assured that your dignity and views will'be treated with the utmost respect and consideration. We dislike using this subterfuge to get to speak with you but it was the only way we could overcome the obstacles of your refusals to meet. We thank you for your consideration and now respectfully await your reply." Joseph cupped his head in his hands and thought long and deep, finally answering, "I confess feeling put out by being trapped into this meeting but understand it was something you had to do, and very cleverly done, I must admit. Before, I say anything, would like Allison to give me her thoughts on this matter." He reached over and taking Allison's hand urged her to respond.

Allison reluctantly spoke, "Joseph, this has to be your decision. I can.t imagine what is involved. I know you feel you have a message to give the world and perhaps this is the means for delivery of your message. I don.t know the motives behind this offer. I can only tell you of my feelings and they are feelings of fear. You are moving out into the world scene and I fear for you and for our love. The world outside of our sheltered habitat is one filled with hate and violence. You will speak of truth and thai will release a torrent of hate and violence. Joseph, I am afraid." Tears filled her eyes. Joseph frowned and reached over to console her. He then turned to Tom. "Sir," he said, "What is the motivation of your company to have me do this interview?" Tom could only stare, while he collected his thoughts, "Why," he said, "It's responding to the public s needs. We are after all, public servants and serving the public. We also have an obligation to let voices, such as yours, bringing important messages to be heard." Joseph smiled, "Is your company a business?" Tom replied, "Yes. I suppose it is." "Is the objective of your company to make a profit?" "Well, the making of a profit is a secondary consideration since that is what keeps us going. Our first consideration is to provide a needed public service of news and communication." Joseph persisted, "You are saying that stock holder dividends, profits, ratings, and advertisement income take a back seat to public service. Do you believe that?" Joseph inquired looking directly at Tom. Tom hesitated, looked down at his feet with a puzzled expression and then collecting himself raised his head and looking directly at Joseph and exclaimed, "No." The silence that followed was heavy and thick. The team members looked at Tom aghast. Tom sat with his head bowed. After a long pause, Joseph spoke, "Tom, I thank you for your courage and honesty. I understand the circumstances that you and your team are in. That survival is involved and I would wish that I could help. If your company was involved with the search for truth, I would agree to the interview. But it, like all others, pursues riches and power to the detriment of all else. I therefore, regretfully, have no choice but to refuse. He shook each hand, bowed and with Allisson, clinging to his arm, they left. In their wake, gloom descended upon the remaining group. They gathered around Tom and assailed him with their questions. How could he do that? What was he thinking? Did he understand he was blowing them out of the water? The entire enterprise and their future was doomed. They demanded answers. Tom with head bowed withstood the barrage of questions in silence. Finally, he lifted his head and replied, "I want to apologize to each of you, that worked so hard to achieve this encounter. I know what I did and I will personally assume all blame for our failure. How do I justify what I did? We are dealing with a very unique individual. When he looked in my eyes, it felt like he was penetrating into my soul and I had to be honest. While this ploy failed, don't be discouraged.

Tomorrow, I call Foster, who told me we had other options that may work. I also will give him all the details of today's encounter and my part in ending it. Let's forget today's setback, get a goodnights sleep and we will meet tomorrow. With these encouraging words, they left.

Early the next morning, Tom called Foster at the home office and was asked to report in person. On arrival Foster listened patiently as Tom described the entire results of their efforts. How they did extensive research on Joseph's background, behavior, and character. How they failed in repeated attempts to speak with him and his complete obstinancy to meeting with them. How they finally arranged, through duplicity, to meet with him and the failed results of that meeting when Tom torpedoed the meeting with his truthful answer. When finished, Tom sat back dejectedly awaiting Foster's reproach. He was startled when Foster commended him and congratulated him on doing superbly in a most difficult situation. Puzzled, he said, "I don't understand, I thought I ruined everything." Foster explained, "On the contrary, you have placed us in a stonger position. When you met with Joseph, his mind was made up. The questions he asked you were only confirmation of what he knew. That you confirmed them with your answer was irrelevant to his decision made before your answer. What you did, my dear Tom, in your eyes was tragic when in actuality it was psychologically very smart. You now have him as your friend. Someone whom he can trust and respect. We now have a member, with influence, in our opponent's camp. This will give our next attempt a greater chance of success. That chances of success were extremely poor. But, we had to try. Now we move on to the next phase that I will explain." Tom sighed with relief. This meeting he had thought would rake him over the coals and perhaps result in his firing, instead he had received praise, unwarranted, he thought, but most welcome. He regarded Foster with appreciation and respect as he listened intently to his proposal. Foster went on, "We know Joseph is immune to most of the normal appeals to human weakness and will not respond to pressure. So we must turn to other avenues that are susceptible to these pressures. That entity is the university itself. Universities are invariably in need of money. Our plan will be to contact the Dean with a substantial monetary donation if he and his faculty, students, and others can persuade Joseph to grant us our desired interview. The pressure they can apply could be so intense that it could force Joseph to comply. The elements of that pressure will not be Joseph's personal inhibitions but the well being of the university. That argument places the entire context in a different light. Not a profit making venture for a TV station but a furtherance of educational benefits for the good of higher values. This plan will require great diligence and effort but I feel has a good chance for success. Tom, I have confidence that you are the best suited for this venture and would like you to take on this task. I, of course, will be supporting you all the way." Tom, elated did not hesitate. "I do accept most gratefully and appreciate your confidence. The longer I know you, the more I learn of your expertise and wisdom and the greater my respect and admiration. Thank you for this opportunity and I will do my best to earn your approval." Foster thanked him and they shook hands. As Tom was preparing to leave, Foster said, "We will meet this afternoon at two and go over the plan, before you leave." They shook hands again and Tom left.

Tom did not leave for two days. Following briefing sessions with Foster, spent one day with family before flying back to Slocum. On his return, he assembled his team to a meeting. They were surprised to find an upbeat, enthusiastic Tom bringing them new expectations instead of the dire news they were expecting. He brought them news of a new approach and that they were being commended for a fine performance. They were overjoyed at what they considered a reprieve and absorbed the enthusiasim that Tom exuded. He then went into details of the plan. "Bill, you will arrange a meeting with the Dean which I and a Mr.Thomas Hall will attend. Mr. Hall is a prominent Alumni of Slocum University, a huge contributor to it and our company stockholder. We have enlisted his support and he has great influence with the school. You can be sure his presence and support will be crucial.

After the introductions and amenities, I will present our proposition. We represent a major national television station and are attempting to respond to a national demand for information of a Slocum student, who has become a figure of national focus. This student, Joseph Stern, has sought anonymity and obscurity from the public scene and obstructed all attempts to respond to public concerns. As public servants, we are duty bond to meet this civic obligation and arrange a broadcast that will satisfy this need. We are prepared to give a sizable donation to Slocum University if they can persuade Joseph to appear at our television station for an interview that will meet the publics demand. This donation will be given to use at the University's discretion, without any restrictions. Bill, depending on Mr.Hall's availability, set up the appointment that we three will attend with the Dean. The rest of you, sit tight, until needed." Finishing they grouped and engaged in excited discussion of their new situation.

A few days, after securing Mr.Hall's availability, Bill called the Dean's office and asked to speak to the Dean on an important matter. Upon reaching the Dean, Bill introduced himself as William Halpern, representing the EGR national television station, and with Mr Thomas Hall and my associate Mr.Thomas Phelps request a meeting of utmost importance to your university. Dean Marcus questioned? Did you say Hall, Thomas Hall?" Bill replied, "Yes, Thomas Hall."

"By all means, anytime Wednesday afternoon if that is acceptable."

"That's fine, we will be there at two. Thank you." Bill reported to Tom that they had an appointment and the time and date. Tom thanked him and said he would arrange Mr.Hall's attendance.

CHAPTER 3

▼

The following Wednesday at two p.m. Tom, Bill and Mr. Hall entered Dean Marcus's office and were greeted by him. He invited them to be seated and had his secretary provide them with coffee. After an exchange of pleasantries, Tom opened the conversation. He started by thanking the Dean for taking time from his busy schedule and giving them an appointment. He then stated the reason for this meeting. "Dean Marcus, I represent the EGR television station and have come here to ask your assistance in arranging an interview on television with a freshman student of yours, a Joseph Stern, and, as you may know, he has achieved national interest. The public is demanding information about him and his views. As public servants, we are obligated to satisfy this demand. All our efforts to entice him to do this interview have failed because of his dislike for publicity and his desire for obscurity. The public clamor for news about him has grown in intensity. We have tried everything to overcome his stubborn refusal. Money, a suitable platform, civic responsibility, hotel and entertainment facilities all have failed, We have come to you as a last resort and as an incentive that may move him to agree, my firm is prepared to give a sizable unconditional donation to your school to benefit your educational goals. Perhaps, his loyalty and dedication to the school will motivate him." He finished, and then Mr. Hall entered the discussion, addressing the Dean by his first name, "Walter, I agree whole heartedly with what EGR is trying to accomplish. I know how these things work at a university. It takes pressure, first get his professors to work on him, then the students, particularly those close to him. I understand he has a student girlfriend. Her help could be enormous. Emphasis should be on helping the school." The Dean nodded in agreement, "This is a worthy project and will follow Mr.Hall's excellent suggestions. A large donation would be most welcome at a time when finances are pressing us." They all got to their feet shook hands and with parting greetings left. Tom and Hill feeling they had done well.

Two weeks later, Joseph was attending Professor William's class. When the class session ended, Professor Williams asked him to remain. After the last student left, Professor Williams shut the door and asked Joseph to be seated near him. He studied Joseph for a moment and then spoke. "Yesterday morning, the Dean met with me and your other class professors. He informed us that you were asked to be interviewed on national television. A request that included monetary and other benefits, which you had refused. He indicated the television station was under considerable public pressure to arrange this interview and had difficulty accepting your refusal to discuss or negotiate. Since various appeals failed to change your mind, they came up with an offer they feel might. They have agreed to establish a trust that will provide scholarships for disadvantaged applicants. Providing educational opportunities for deserving finanacially-deprived students could be the incentive for your cooperation. The Dean was delighted with this proposal and has asked us to use our influence to persuade you. I am reluctant to pressure you on this matter. If you choose to discuss this with me, I will do it not as advocate for the Dean but as your friend." Joseph sat back and looked at the Professor. "How can I ever thank you for your kindness to me. I feel as though I am in a whirlpool with things pulling me this way and that. There are so many pressures. You give me a sense of security and stability. I am so grateful and I would like to talk this out and have your opinion." Professor Williams smiled, "O.K.

let's talk this out. I know you have a message to give to the world. It seems that being on a national television would be a splendid opportunity to deliver such a message. Why did you refuse?" Joseph shook his head, "Because I don't trust their motives. I am sure they won't put me on for the sake of my delivering a message but rather to create a situation of confrontation and chaos. They want something to promote their ratings and profits and I know they would use me in such a way as .to benefit them and perhaps destroy me in the process. Television today has perverted news, truth, and morality in favor of sex and entertainment. News is packaged so it becomes entertainment with falsely created suspense and eye-catching violence. Frankly, I am afraid of its exposure." Professor Williams took some time before speaking, "I understand your reservations. What you say about today's television is all too true. I am not prepared to give you an opinion now. I will need time. I must warn you. You will be subjected to tremendous pressure to change. All the forces of the university will be arrayed against you. I am sure you will be confiding with Allison. Listen to her. Sometimes women have a better feel for this sort of thing then men do. They sense some things we do not. I will discuss this with you later, meanwhile, be strong." Joseph's thoughts turned to Allison.

He headed to the cafeteria and their usual meeting place. Allison was waiting for him. After obtaining their food and being seated, Joseph opened the discussion. He told her of his meeting with Professor Williams and the pressure the Dean requested be applied to change Joseph's mind. The television station would donate a large sum to the university if they got Joseph to change his mind. The professor had warned him to be prepared for pressure from faculty and students, that the entire university would be turned against him. Allison looked at him with sympathy, "You are right. My language professor told me, she heard I had a close relation with you and that for the good of the school, I should ask you to agree to their request. I told her I would talk to you. You know whatever you decide, I would support you." Joseph replied, "I know that and I greatly appreciate it. I felt so right and positive in my actions, but now there is uncertainty, confusion as to direction. I know you don't want to affect my thinking, but I am asking you to give me whatever insight you have that might help my dilemma." Allison reflected for some time and then gave voice to her thoughts.

"Alright, I will tell you what I feel. Sometime ago, I said, I felt as though a giant hand was turning a wheel of your destiny towards a determined goal. All the events that have happened to you seem to be moving you, despite your strenuous objections, towards that eventuality. Some strange, incomprehensible force is working its will on you. You objected to coming to this university and you were persuaded to go. You objected to appearing on the panel discussion and were persuaded to go. You objected to becoming a public figure and was forced to accept it. You were offered a spot on national television which you rejected and are now being pressured to accept. The wheel is being turned by a giant hand and is inexorably leading you to its destination. I know you will be forced to accept and that will put you on the world stage where you will speak truths and bring a torrent of hate and I know not what other ills it will bring you. I don't know if this force moving you plans you as a sacrifice or if it will use its powers to protect you. I have this terrible fear for you. I pray it is wrong." She stopped and looked at him with her love pouring from her eyes and then burst into heavy weeping. Distraught, Joseph seized her, hugged and kissed her and sought to comfort her. They held each other tightly until her sobbing stopped and she gaining her composure tried to apologize but Joseph would not allow it. Holding her tightly, he would only repeat his love and devotion to her. They collected themselves and prepared to leave, ignoring the audience of student on-lookers watching. Walking to the entrance and before leaving, Joseph said, "You have given me a lot to think about and I will give it a great deal of thought," With a goodbye embrace, he left.

Later that afternoon, he had a visitor. It was Phillip Haber the student class president. There was no need for introduction since they had become acquainted earlier. He had entered Joseph's quarters and was invited to be seated. Phillip immediately explained the purpose of his meeting. "Joseph.I am sure you know that a large funding project that will be of extreme benefit to the school is being made providing you consent to a television interview. The Dean has requested that you be informed, by me, that the entire student body is whole heartedly for this project and that you are urged to make its consummation possible. Your agreement will earn the gratitude of your Alma Mater and the gratitude of countless future deprived students. You need not reply immediately, but please give it your utmost consideration. He then shook his hand and departed. Leaving Joseph buried in thought.

The next day Joseph presented himself at Professor Williams's office. He seated himself on the chair offered and thanked the professor for seeing him. "Professor Williams, I find myself in a quandary and could use some help." He then related his conversation with Allison and with the class president, Phillip Haber.". I know the pressure is just beginning and will become unbearable. Allison feels I am fighting forces that cannot be resisted and I should allow it to take its course. She hopes it will protect me. I could use your advice as to what to do." Professor Williams frowned with concern. "Joseph, your position is most difficult. I share your concern that the interview will not be favorable to you. That you will be used for their purpose. Allison perceives a force at work here that may nullify their plans and place you in authority. I am skeptical but her vision may be more accurate than mine. the choices are dismal. To become a pariah at your school or a victim of the media. Hesitantly, I recommend the latter and may good fortune be with you." He finished and shook his head sadly. Thanking him Joseph left.

The next morning, Joseph awoke late after a sleepless night. He had turned and tossed all night as his mind revolved around the decision being forced on him. Still drowsy he had come to a conclusion which he made known to Professor Williams at the end of class. He had decided to agree to the interview. Professor said he felt it was the only reasonbable answer and wished him good fortune. Joseph then sent word to Tom Phelps that he would like to have him come to his room at the end of classes. Tom accepted and felt encouraged by that request. At five p.m. Tom knocked on Joseph's door and was admitted by Joseph. Jack, who had been studying, gathered up his books and evidently, by prior agreement, left the room leaving Tom alone with Joseph. After shaking hands in greeting, Tom sat in a chair offered by Joseph and waited for him to speak. Joseph was seated facing Tom and spoke directly to him. "As you probably guessed I have called you to give you my decision on the interview. I have decided reluctantly and with much misgivings to agree to it. I do so because the pressures brought about by your company have overwhelmed me. You were able to enlist the entire university and other elements in this campaign to bend me to your will. Unwillingly, I have now capitulated. This undoubtedly is a feather in your cap and may earn you a promotion or bonus. That would please me. If that sounds strange, I will explain. Tom, I respect you as an honest man and I like you. As a realist, I know your obligations of family care and support are your priority and earning a living requires playing by the current rules of the game. I am sure that you strive to be ethical and so if my actions bring you a bene-fit, that pleases me. You have dealt with me fairly and with respect. I appreciate your behavior and would like to consider you a friend."

He stopped and looked at Tom. Tom felt overcome by emotion and could hardly speak. When he did he had to clear his throat. "Joseph, when I came here, I thought I knew you had decided to give in. I was prepared for anger and abuse. Instead, I find you regard me as a friend, despite the anguish our actions have caused you. Knowing your values, I always held you in high esteem and regretted doing the job required. Now that you are committed, as your friend, I want to warn you of the pitfalls that you will encounter. Trust no one in my company. When I told my people of our exchange, they said, I had made you as a friend and they now had me as a spy for their side. I want you to know that as your friend, I will be your spy in their camp and will alert you to their plans for you." Joseph warmly shook his hand with both of his, "I am most grateful for your friendship and will need all the help you can give."

The following day, Tom and his team returned to their home office. He reported to Foster the news of their success. Foster was overjoyed at the news and after congratulating Tom and his team, wasted no time in reporting it to his boss, Alvin Tucker. Tucker was pleased and told Foster to call a meeting of the Board and staff for the next morning to formulate plans for the interview. He indicated the interview should take place as soon as possible.as events made its immediate release most advantageous, Foster indicated his prompt compliance.

The next morning the full board of the EGR Corporation met with designated staff members to discuss the arrangements for the forthcoming interview with Joseph. The Board chairman, Mr.Alvin Tucker sat at the head off the table and opened the meeting for discussion with his statement, "This is a very important meeting. We have met to discuss the arrangements for interviewing Joseph Stern on our station. But first, I want to congratulate Sid Foster, Tom Phelps and his team for a very difficult job. Well done. My review of the events leading up to his final consent informed me of the almost impossible obstacles they overcame. Their effort is a credit to their abilities and the efficacy of our company. Now on the subject of this interview. It comes at a most auspicious time for us. Currently there is a lapse of interest gripping events on the national and international scene. Political turmoil is unusually dormant. The world of entertainment and sports is temporarilly devoid of shock and scandal. Internationally there is no great catastrophies or nation upheavals to command attention. The public is hungry for some item that will rouse them from the mundane and boring into flaming emotions of feelings and excitement. This characteristic of human nature must be understood in developing successful marketing stragety and explains why people, who can barely scratch out a living, are deeply concerned with the intimate details of the lives of rich and famous. We now have an opportunity, with this Joseph

Stern, to create an event that may arouse a storm of interest, discussion and controversy that may involve all segments of our national population, and even some international involvement. How we handle this may be a boon or a disaster to our station. It must be done exactly right so that it reflects real benfit to our studio. We have people with the skill and expertise to develop the right approach. I will now throw it open to your best analysis and approach. Anyone that wants to speak will be welcome. I will start by asking Sid Foster, who has set up the team effort that achieved this interview, to give us what they have learned about this Joseph." Foster rose to his feet and said, "My knowledge is limited except for what has been said about him in the press and by others. That he claims to be a prophet and was given a message by God to deliver to humanity. I would like to turn this over to Tom Phelps, who has done extensive research on Joseph and had close personal contact with him and his views. He also succeded in overcoming his objections to the interview.

As Tom got up to speak, he received lengthy applause from the group. Smiling and with thanks, Tom acknowledged the ovation. He then spoke. "We are dealing with a very unique individual. Joseph does not fit the usual mode of evangelical type. He believes he was commanded by some unseen force to deliver a message of truth to the world. He does not claim to be speaking for God, since he doesn.t believe in our version of a personal God. He does not claim to be a prophet or have supernatural powers derived from heaven. He believes he does have the ability to see truth and reality as opposed to what he considers man.s arrogance in creating a universe dedicated to gratifying the desires of the human race. He is truly a humble man with no interest in wealth or position but weighted down with the burden of an ordained mission to present the truth to a misguided world. He feels his message will release a storm of hate and violence directed at him. He dreads it but it will not deter him. He seeks no rewards, monetary or approbation. His desire is peace and privacy." He sat down with his listeners reacting with deep silence and troubling thoughts. The silence continued for an interminably long time and was finally broken by Mr.Tucker." This is a unique situation because of the uniquess of the individual. Evidently, it will have to be handled with kid gloves. Perhaps, Mr.Green, our marketing director can give some direction." Mr.Green spoke, "This is a difficult marketing problem. First, we must decide what is best to further the interests of our station. Secondly, how to respond adequately and satisfactorily to the public clamor. Thirdly, how to protect our station from a destructive public response. Joseph indicated that when he spoke the truth it could release a torrent of hate and violence. If his truth attacks organized religion, or public policy and behavior, regardless of the truth and validity of his remarks, we can be sure many groups, I can't define the size or number, will rise up with hate and even violence. There are certain things that are secret to many believers. These beliefs go to the core of a persons being. Attack them and you are in effect destroying them. This will not be tolerated regardless of logic. Reason, evidence, or even benefits. If your mother is being attacked, regardless of the reason, logic, or justification, you would strike back with a vengeance. The same is true of beliefs cherished from childhood that become part of a person's psychic. Gifted individuals of superior intellect and education still adhere to doctrines of childhood they do not discard despite all evidence that negates them. As a public station, we dare not put ourselves in a position that we support or endorse the views he may express. A resulting backlash could end up in a disastrous boycutt of our station. Our position must not only be completely neutral but perhaps slightly in opposition so that we are protected." Mr.Tucker took the floor. "I want to thank John for a masterful presentation. I think his analysis and the action required is right on target. He has very clearly defined the risks and the direction we must take in arranging this interview. Our goal must be to give this Joseph an opportunity to express his views but our interviewers must conduct it in a manner that will emphasize our strict neutrality and our support for public concerns. "Does anyone want to express a view or opinion?" Receiving no response, he declared the meeting closed and instructed Foster to meet with Mr. Green and work out the details as to individuals conducting the interview and the format of the interview.

Foster and John Green left together for Mr.Green's office. They had asked Tom Phelps to join them in discussing arrangements for the interview. After establishing a tentative time and date for the interview, they then tackled selection of the interviewers and the direction and conduct of the interview. Foster and Green agreed that the station should declare its neutrality and a disclaimer for any responsibility for views presented, while announcing its support for cherished public beliefs. The interviewers should challenge any statements that might violate public sensibilities. And seek to maintain a moderate civil tone to the proceedings. Foster then asked Tom for his views and if he would consent to be an interviewer. He told Tom, his experience with Joseph and his proven abilities made Tom his first choice for an interviewer. Tom expressed his appreciation for this high regard, but respectfully declined stating that the pressure he had put on Joseph might produce a discordant and harmful element to the interview. Foster understood and agreed but wanted Tom to still be a party to the planning, to which Tom agreed. He also agreed to be the go-between the station and Joseph. After much discussion, two individuals were selected. One, a Mr.Duane Walters, the station's noted interviewer and his assistant Wilbur Holmes, were selected and briefed as to the format. The selections and the entire format was then submitted to Mr. Alvin Tucker for final approval. Upon receiving approval, Tom was advised to make arrangements for transportation and suitable accommodations. At Tom's insistence adjoining hotel rooms, dining, and entertainment expense were authorized for Allison and Joseph's parents. When Tom called Joseph and notified him of the time and date of his interview and that arrangements had been made for Allison and his parents to be with him. Joseph was overjoyed. He told Tom, "I know you have gone to great trouble to arrange this. I would be lost without Allison and my parents were planning to come, at their own expense, to meet Allison and to attend the interview. You are truly a dear friend." Tom replied, "I was delighted I could do this for you. When settled, we must have a talk. You are about to enter the lion's cage. We must try to defang him. I will meet you on your arrival and escort you to your hotel, meanwhile be of good spirits."

CHAPTER 4

▼

One week later, Joseph and Allison arrived. They were met by Tom, who escorted them to their hotel. His parents had arrived a day earlier and were eagerly waiting to hear from him. Joseph decided they would all meet for dinner in the hotel dining room and invited Tom and his wife to join them. Tom had to refuse, since living out of town, time did not permit acceptance on such short notice. With fond farewells and a promise to get together in the near future, Tom left. Joseph then called his parents to inform them of their arrival and suggested they get together in their room, prior to dinner for greetings and introductions. They were very anxious to see him and meet his girl friend and so an early time was set. At the designated time, Joseph knocked on his parent's door and entered with Allison. Both parents greeted him with hugs and kisses and he then introduced Allison. They greeted her affectionately and his mother complimented on his choice of so attractive a young lady. Joseph said, "Yes mom, she is beautiful but I am going to marry her for her mind. When you get to know her you will find she is as beautiful inside as outside." His father said, "I am sure you are right but now lets head for the dining room in case that inside needs some nourishment," They all laughed and collecting themselves left for the dining room.

Seated at a lavish table, they engaged in light conversation. Joseph's parents were very interested in Allison and questioned her about family and early background. Allison responded quietly and courtesly. The only serious question they asked, what did she think of Joseph's current situation? Her reply that she supported Joseph in all his decisions without any reservations impressed them. She obviously made a good first impression and as time went on their affection for Allison increased. During the course of the dinner there was entertainment and dancing, in which they all participated. At a fairly late hour, they decided to leave and headed for their rooms. Before departing Joseph's father spoke to him, "We have had conversations on the phone, but now things have reached a point, I feel the need to have a very serious talk about what you are heading into. I have grave concerns about it I would appreciate if you could arrange a time for me." Joseph said, "I would be happy to meet with you and hear you out.if following breakfast tomorrow suits you. I will be available." His father said, "That's fine, we have a date." They parted with a hug. Josreph then escorted Allison to her door. Saying goodnight, he hugged and kissed her passionately. Their embrace and kissing grew more heated. He finally broke off and whispered my passion for you is becoming unbearable, I want to make love to you, to adore and worship you, to devour you, I lust for you. When this thing is finished, we must get married, I don't want to wait." Allison, with tears in her eyes, said, "I have those same feelings, but wait we must and I pray that won't be long." With the words, "I love you," he released her and she entered her room.

The next morning, after breakfast, Joseph went to his father's room. His father greeted him warmly and they sat together on the sofa. The mother was occupied elsewhere, so the two were alone. The father opened the conversation. "Joseph, we were astonished at the sudden notoriety you achieved. All at once the newspapers were carrying articles about you. They were publishing stories; I could not believe and as you told me on the phone, were not true. That you were a prophet who spoke to God. That you were carrying a message to the world that came directly from God. Now you will be presented on national television to present your message. I have fears about this forthcoming interview that I want you to hear.and consider. "He stopped and looked at Joseph. Joseph replied, "Dad, you know I hold you in the highest esteem. I respect your wisdom and your views. I am very aware that we are dealing with extremely serious and perhaps dangerous matters. I would appreciate hearing any input of yours and will give it most serious consideration." His father then spoke, "Fine, these are my thoughts. I don't know what you will be saying or the interrogation you will be receiving and how you will reply but I would like you to keep this in mind. You are a member of a tiny minority, the Jewish people. For thousands of years we have clung to our faith despite countless unceasing efforts throughout those years to eliminate us. We have withstood the test of time and hate. We have witnessed mighty empires, rule the world and then fade into oblivion, while we survived. Survived because we adapted to circumstance without abandoning our moral and religious beliefs. You are about to appear on the national scene. You may say things that some will consider attacking deep held religious or traditional beliefs. To those who respond to any difference with hate, you will not be considered an individual with a differing viewpoint but a Jew. Presenting doctrines of that cursed race and justify adding fuel to a growing field of anti-semitism. As you know in Judaism, there are a hundred differing interpretations, but the world lumps it all into one basket of obstinate and deceitful behavior. These are my concerns that you realize, your words may be seen as the words of all our people." He finished and looked sadly at Joseph. Joseph frowned and said, "Dad.I have thought long and hard about these things you mention. The message I hope to present is a message that seeks to recognize truth. It is not my intention to attack any religious beliefs; I know how dangerous that could be. And I will not present myself as having any heavenly message. The reality of truth is all about us and only needs recognition. I hope to bring that reality into view. The present direction of the human race is towards self-destruction, and it needs a wake up call. Not to rouse up animosity and discordance but to bring to us the realization that time is running out. Corrective action must be taken now. We hope it is not too late." Following his statement there was silence. A troubled mood descended on them. After a lengthy pause, his father spoke. "I don't comprehend the forces moving you. When you first came to us with what I considered an inconsequential dream and your foolish intention to carry out its message. I decided to play along with it. The turn of events has caused me to change. These events have brought you recognition and placed you on the world stage. I now regard you, my son, with a sense of awe. The clarity of your vision and speech reach far beyond your age, I feel something in you is beyond human normality and I tremble to think that you may be the instrument of some higher power and how it may use you. There is so much mystery in our life and the universe that surrounds us. There is so much the human mind cannot comprehend. We seek answers but our met with silence. Only charlatans' answers, who claim God speaks to them. You may have been given some answers that you are able to impart. I can only offer our love, support, and prayers for you as you prepare your answers." Joseph answered his father with an embrace. "Dad," he said. "Your love and support mean everything to me. In a few days I will be on the 'hot seat' and having you, mom, and my beloved Allison there supporting me, will give me the strength to behave in a way that, I hope, will bring honor to you." With another fond embrace, Joseph departed.

CHAPTER 5

▼

The day of the interview finally arrived. Extensive preparations had been made. The session would be held in a larger studio to accommodate the many attending. Requests for reporter attendance from several major national media firms had been granted as well as for several international media reporters. Representatives from some major religious, civic, and political organizations had also been approved for attendance. Joseph's parents, Allison, along with important personages who had applied would also attend. The front seats were reserved for Joseph's parents, Allison, and the studio company executives that included Alvin Tucker, Sid Foster, Tom Phelps and their wives. The studio was a massive clutter of wiring, lamps, photo and projection equipment and microphones. The stage was set with a curtain background. A large table fitted with three chairs, two at one side for the two interviewers, and one at the other end for Joseph. Each chair was provided with a microphone. The technicians had arrived early and were busy connecting and setting up their equipment. Soft classical music provided background as the studio gradually filled. The time had been set for ten AM. At ten minutes earlier, the two interviewers entered the stage and took their seats. They brought with them several files and literature they placed on the table. They checked the microphones and then engaged in conversation with each other. They both were dressed in conventional business attire with ties. Duane Walters, the senior member, middle aged, distinguished looking and wore spectacles. His assistant Wilbur Holmes was much younger, in his thirties. At this time, Joseph entered and before taking his seat, bowed to the brief and scattered applause, he received.

The time for the interview arrived. The audience had settled in their seats and there was utter silence as Duane Walters made his opening statement. Looking directly into the TV camera, he announced the station and welcomed the public to the viewing of this national and international event. He then introduced himself, his assistant Wilbur Holmes as the interviewers and then Joseph Stern as the subject of the interview. In his opening speech, he made this statement. "This interview has been arranged by your EGR station in response to public demand for information about Joseph Stern and the message he brings to the world from God. The Station wishes to make crystal clear that it does not endorse or support any statement by Mr.Stern that conflicts with any religious, political or traditional belief of any recognized group. That any statement he makes that is not acceptable to the general public is strictly his own, individualistic opinion and is not supported by our policy of protecting the rights and beliefs of the public. With that understood disclaimer, we will now proceed with the interview."

He then turned to Joseph and said, "Joseph, you are most welcome and we express our appreciation for your agreeing to appear for this interview that we trust will enlighten our viewers. "My first question-we have been told that you consider yourself a prophet, do you truly make that claim? Joseph shook his head. "No, I have never considered or claimed to be a prophet. I don't know how that story developed." You claim there is no basis for that, but surely, there must have been something that gave that story its impetus. Do you have any clue?" There is something, I had this very vivid dream. In my dream, a powerful voice spoke to me, it said, "Joseph, you have the gift of the prophecy of truth.go forth and prophecy truth throughout the land. Well then, Joseph, doesn't that make you a prophet?"

"Not to me. The dictionary defines a prophet as one who can foretell future events and happenings. To prophecies truth is defining something that already exists. I never claimed to have the ability to predict the future."

"You say a heavenly voice spoke to you in your dream, was that the voice of God? Joseph shook his head, "No."

"Whose voice was it?"

"I don't know"

"If you don't know, why do you deny it couldn't be God,"

"I don't believe God talks to humans."

"Why not? You believe in God, don't you?" Joseph shook his head, "No." A shocked murmur spread through the audience. With raised voice Duane Walters almost shouted at Joseph. "You don't believe in God?"

Joseph replied. "I believe there could be a creator, but not the personal God humans have created to satisfy their needs, that is fantasy." Still with raised voice Duane railed, "You don't believe in a God of love and forgiveness?" Joseph said, "No. I believe in the laws of the universe that you can ascribe to anyone you choose, demands justice and truth for survival, not love. If one thousand people are dying of cancer and all pray to the loving God for remission so they can live and one is blessed with a remission you will say that one person's recovery was an example of prayer answered. The rest unanswered die."

There was a pause, then Walters said, "Some would say that was a miracle. Do you believe in miracles?"

"No"Joseph replied, "A miracle is a violation of nature's laws. I don't believe nature violates its own laws. Unusual events related to us from ancient times and more recent times may be due to causes beyond our knowledge."

"I suppose you don't believe in a soul or eternal life?"

"My opinion is no. Let me stress that is my current opinion. My mind has trouble accepting the idea that in a universe of billions of galaxies, containing trillions of planets and stars, this microscopic dot of earth is favored above all else. I seek truth, and this is my truth. I also realize there are unknown dimensions that exist in this amazing universe beyond our comprehension that could prove me wrong. So my mind is open to any new fact that proves me wrong."

The interviewers held a brief dicussion and then Duane Walters turned the session over to his assistantWilbur Holmes. He opened up the questioning, "Mr.Stern, despite your objections, things you have indicated seemed to support your assumption that you do have discourse with spiritual beings. Would you care to describe them."

"I don't know what you are talking about."

"Well, you describe their voices perhaps you can give us an inkling of their attire. Is it modern wear or perhaps 13 or 14 century costume or perhaps very ancient wear?"

"I have never seen them."

"There is an implication that you were perhaps speaking with God.In biblical literature, the presence of God is marked by some physical manifestation. I refer to Moses and the burning bush as an example. Did anything like that take place?"

Joseph angrily answered, "No."

"You deny having prophetic powers to foretell the future but surely your contacts with your spiritual mentors must give you some ability in that dirction that your modesty denies, As a minor matter could you give a forecast on our economic future, the stock market?"

His face turning red, Joseph responded, "I am not an economist, I know nothing of that."

Wilbur Holmes shuffled and studied some papers lying in front of him. Turning again to Joseph framed another question. "Today, with the world in turmoil, with conflict and dissension everywhere, many religions feel the predictions of Armageddon are coming to pass and the approach of the messiah who will liberate us all from the woes of this planet are about to happen. Surely you, who may be our last prophet, and confidant of spiritual beings, can give us the long awaited prediction as to the coming of the Messiah. Do not deny us and give us our long awaited and desired answer."

Joseph, in a rage, rose to his feet. With a sweep of his hands he cleared the table sending all its contents crashing to the floor. His eyes, wide and glaring flamed into the television cameras and his voice roaring filled the room. "You mock me," his voice blasted. "You mock me for a prophecy. You shall have it. I make prophesy to you and the world regarding the prophesy of the coming of the Messiah.

> TheMessiah comes but not to bring true believers,
> The anointed to a heavenly paradise,
> He comes wearing the mask of the face of death.
> To eliminate the human race from the planet
> Since they are wicked and evil.
> Violent and cruel without mercy.
> They violate nature's laws of survival
> By murdering their own species
> They create gods of love and forgiveness
> They say destroy those who do not accept me.
> Man preaches love and practices hate.
> In a garden of Eden, a paradise planet.
> Unique in the universe.
> Turned into a poisonous desert.
> By contaminating humans
> From the tree of life, the fruit greed and hate.
> An arrogance that has no limits
> Overpopulation the planet cannot support.
> Environmental destruction without limit.
> Destruction of species without concern

Conciliatory to ruling tyrants using violence
To exploit their poverty, ignorant people,
Doers of evil, a sentence awaits you...
A harsh judgement of the Universe.
The flaming sword of retribution
Unsheathed, and handed to nature
Striking with exterminating calamities
Humans. Idle spectators at the race. Between
Nature and man's weapons of mass destruction
As to who wins our extinction
A terrible storm gathers that the comfort
Of our homes will not protect.

Joseph finished. The audience sat in silence; no one applauded or said a word. No one spoke. Joseph got up and left the stage. He did not speak to anyone, but went to the side of the stage and waited for his parents and Allison. They met and wordlessly left together. The only break was when Tom Phelps waved to him.

CHAPTER 6

▼

Early that evening, Joseph and Allison went to his parent's room. They had planned an evening dinner with Tom and his wife, Dorothy.Joseph's parents would be leaving for home, in the morning. Upon entering, Joseph and Allison made themselves comfortable on the sofa and were joined by his parents. The heavy silence that affected them after Joseph's words still controlled them. Joseph's father looked depressed, finally he spoke, "Joseph the message you gave was a terrible condemnation of the human race. You may have unleashed forces that will strike back with ferocity. You claim to bring truths that the world must recognize. Historically the world rejects truths and rejects those who bring it, Galileo and others, for example. I cannot fault you. You are being motivated by elements beyond my comprehension. Your mother and I can only pray no harm will come to you. We are certain that Allison, who loves you, has the same concerns and she should speak. Allison said, "You are right, I have great fears. No matter what happens I will be at his side as long as I live. I support him in everything he does." Joseph thanked his parents and responded to Allison with an embrace.

Later that evening they entered the dining room and were met by Tom Phelps and his wife Dorothy. After introductions they were seated at a lavish table and Joseph ordered wine. When the cups were filled and toasts were made, Joseph gave his father a detailed account of Tom's role and the help and friendship, he had received from Tom. His father thanked Tom and then asked him, what he thought of the interview? Tom responded. "I thought he handled it very well. They had set it up to make a caricature of Joseph and he turned that effort against them. When in desperation they sought to mock him, he brought the roof down on them. The substance of his prophecy was a bombshell that may have repercussions worldwide. Unfortunately, every word is true. But more unfortunately, very few will want to accept that as truths but only an attack on the untruths that are cherished and control them. What do I believe? I believe Joseph is a true prophet." When he finished, Joseph got up and walked over to Tom, Tom rose and Joseph shook his hand and gave him a hug.

The conversation took a lighter turn. They talked about events at home, early days and their problems growing up, incidents at their schools and those at the university. Joseph talked about professor Williams and what a benefactor he had become. The social; contacts and odd characters they had known. The orchestra was playing enticing dance music and they engaged in periodic dancing. During a respite as they were all seated, engaged in conversating and indulging in their wine, they were distracted by a slight disturbance. A middle-aged lady, extremely well-dressed and, obviously tipsy, had stood up and pointing her finger, shouted, "There he is. There's Joseph!" A gentleman with her tried to control her, she broke away from and striding to Joseph's table, yelled, "You want to destroy us," seizing a glass of wine from the table, splashed it into his face. She was immediately surrounded by several men who hustled her away. The management and waiters came with apologies and clean up. Joseph wiped the wine from his face, and sat silent and dejected. Tom spoke, "Joseph.you are going to be hit with many such violations of uncivilized behavior. Be strong. Remember you are right and they are wrong. The road you chose to travel is difficult and requires great stength and courage. Complete and utter belief in yourself is demanded. Remember there are countless numbers who will believe in you and your mission." Joseph looked up and said, "Thank you, my true and loyal friend."

Two days after Joseph's parents left. Joseph and Allison returned to their university and resumed their studies but the atmosphere was different. Students no longer showed their former cordiality but appeared to have a guarded and restrained attitude. While a few students congratulated Joseph on his TV appearance as expressing long needed truths, a majority were troubled and disturbed by the impact of his presentation. Joseph sought out Professor Williams.He was eager to get his reaction to the event. Entering his office, after class, Joseph apologized for the intrusion, which was waved away as Professor Williams declared his pleasure at his visit. He told Joseph, he knew why he came and he was anxious to review what happened with him. He told Joseph, "I think your handling of an effort to make you serve their purpose was masterful. Your final prophecy was colossal. The brutal current truths you exposed and declared will not be accepted but will be denied over and over again. But denials will not alter the progression of these truths. Denials will not alter the doom of the human race. I believe you are truly a prophet.ordained by what source, I cannot imagine. That is a mystery and your destiny is a mystery. I can only offer you my support and belief in you. Your way will be hard and perhaps I can help." With these words Professor Williams stood up and shook Jopseph's hand.

CHAPTER 7

▼

Early the next morning, a delegation that had a scheduled appointment with the Dean, arrived. They were cordially welcomed by Dean Marcus. The delegation consisted of eight members, including three alumni, and was headed by a Spencer Hawthorne. They represented a conservative group, concerned with the views expressed by Joseph in his broadcast interview. Mr. Hawthorne explained the purpose of their visit. "Dean Marcus," he began, "as a group that includes many of your university supporters and that places great importance on American values and beliefs, we were outraged by the inflammatory remarks and outright distortions of root principles of our traditional beliefs. His words give ammunition to those whose chief desire is to destroy the foundations of our government.and replace it with world government that would exploit sex and immorality. We recommend that it would serve the best interests of your school to expel this Joseph Stern and the radical movement he represents." He ended and looked at the dean with anticipation. Dean Marcus tapped a pencil on his desk top, while reflecting on his reply. He finally spoke, "Gentlemen, I can understand your concern as to the views this Joseph expressed. I can readily acknowledge that those views conflict with mine and with the majority of the university. However, I must point out that the university is a supporter of free speech. A liberal policy of most universities and is in accordance with the first amendment of the Constitution of the United States. We can contradict, challenge, oppose statements we differ with but cannot deny students the right to express themselves. To do so could make us liable for legal redress Debate and a free exchange of ideas is a necessary part of the educational process. I trust you will understand that the university policy requires me to respectfully deny your request." Mr.Hawethorne responded with some heat, "I do not understand. At a time when our nation is under siege. It's values shredded and stamped on. When sex, homoxexuality, atheism, immorality, and anti-religion is rampant. When the strident voices of the godless overwhelms. We are allowing these worms of our destruction eat away the fabric of a moral society. We don't understand but accept your decision and hope it does not detract from your status, they left without a handshake.

After they were gone, the dean's secretary called the student editor and gave him a full account of the meeting and its result. The student editor thanked her and said that report would get full coverage in the next publication of the student school paper. A week later the story was published and created a great deal of excitement among the students. They were ecstatic that the dean had come out so strongly in support of their right to free speech and the free exchange of ideas. They were extremely laudatory of the dean's actions and help manifest a change in their attitude towards Joseph.Whom they now felt had a right to express his views. The local newspaper also picked up on the story and gave it coverage.

Joseph was receiving a flood of mail and calls. A prominent evangilist, who preached to thousands called Joseph and told him he had received a message from God, saying that Joseph was the messiah and inviting him to attend a meeting for that announcement. Joseph had declined. He also declined other invitations by environmentalists and other groups, who supported himHe refused to answer any mail or attend any invited function but tried to surround himself in a shelter of privacy. While some of the letters supported him, the majority were vitriolic and brimming with hatred. Some even suggested that he should be removed and it would be a blessing if he were gone.

Some time later, as Joseph was walking to class, a student yelled at him, "Hey, Joseph, take a look outside, your fan club is gathered there." Joseph left for a vantage point where he could observe a large gathering at the entrance to the university. A huge demonstration was taking place. Large banners proclaimed, "JOSEPH IS EVIL, NOT THE HUMAN RACE," another "LOVE RULES THE WORLD NOT YOUR HATE." There were many similar banners all proclaiming a venomous dislike of Joseph. Speakers with loud speakers were urging the demonstraters on with vocal expressions and led them in songs that expressed opposition to Joseph's views. Shocked and depressed by the size and volume of the demonstration against him, Joseph felt that perhaps Professor Williams could help restore his composure. Professor Williams was solicitous. He told Joseph, this was a reaction he feared. His message misunderstood, rejected would foster hate and we hope, no violence. He said, "Joseph, be warned. We hope no violence towards you but forces have been released whose direction cannot be determined. Make your personal safety your utmost concern. Be wary of strangers and group contacts. Have no regular schedules that can define your appearances. Be erratic. Meet Allison at unscheduled times and places and not isolated. Take every precaution with eyes and ears alert to unusual events or circumstance. Be constantly alert. This above all else, feel complete in the righteousness of your message and the truths disclosed, never doubt yourself. Be brave, be strong. Remember, I am your friend and I love you." Sadly he got up and hugged Joseph.

One evening a group of eight men, met at the private home of Michael Avon. In a secluded room of that house they were seated around a large table. Several lit candles were the only illumination provided in the room. Lying on the table were a gun and a Bible. The meeting was opened by Michael Avon, the chairman, who said, "I warmly welcome your appearance here to inaugurate our group to be known as the 'Angels of the Righteous.' Our purpose is to oppose those who would remove a beneficent God from our society. Recently, we had some success but now we are faced with a growing threat that needs to be stopped. I refer to this supposed prophet, Joseph Stern, who has prophesized that the human race is evil and will be destroyed by this same beneficent God, who has nurtured and protected us with his love for countless generations. He even questions the existence of a heavenly ruler, as we know Him and His attitude towards His devoted subjects, this is completely unacceptable and should be ignored. Unfortunately, there are many individuals who sit in the shadow of doubt and are vulnerable to this message. This belief in the unsuitability of the human race to survive and questioning of the divine gift of immortality must be opposed and stopped. But how? In life, when confronted by a cancerous tumor, surgery is called for that removes the cancerous growth and allows life to go on. This Joseph Stern is a cancerous growth that also must be removed to save society and our way of life. While we oppose violence, it like surgery has its moment of need. We cannot allow our strong opposition to violence to detract us from our obligations and duty to mankind. We must be strong and sacrifice our principles against violence to a higher principal that requires it. As members of this organization and dedicated to its purpose you will be required to take a sacred oath on this sacred bible and weapon, swearing loyalty to our organization and to comply with any of its rulings, We will now take a vote. All those in favor of taking the prescribed oath, please raise your hand." All present raising their hands, the oath taking ritual was begun. Each member stepped forward and placing one hand on the bible and the other on the gun took the oath swearing loyalty to the organization and to carry out all its orders, without question, when the ritual was completed, the chairman then made a motion that Joseph would be eliminated and that two members, selected by lot, would perform the execution, With all business completed, the meeting was adjourned and the planning for Joseph's execution began.

Two nights later, Joseph had fallen into a troubled sleep. The turmoil caused by the interview was increasing in intensity, not only nationally, but worldwide as well. A flood of support was gaining ground but an even much greater flow of hate and disenssion was evident. All of this was very distressing and depressing to Joseph, who only wished for privacy, tranquility and Allison. Finally, falling asleep exhausted, he was in a deep slumber when a loud stentorian voice broke into his dream, "David, David," it called. In his dream Joseph responded, "I am not David, I am Joseph." The voice continued, "David, David, beware the curse of Saul, Flee, David," Joseph in his dream cried out "I am Joseph, not David." The voice faded away. "Go, Go," Joseph awoke wet with perspiration. What had happened? Why David? Why Saul? What did it mean? He remembered the story in the Old Testament. How King Saul pursued David with passionate vengeance in his desire to kill David. Was this a warning? That his death at the hands of an assassin was imminent? Dare he wait? He felt an urgency to respond and thought of calling Allison.

CHAPTER 8

▼

Wasting no time he called Allison and asked her to meet him immediately at the entrance to her dormitory. He rushed there and found her waiting. Then he related to her, his dream. He felt might be a warning and asked her advice." Allison replied, "Joseph, since your interview, I have lived in dread of what might threaten you. There is a growing intensity of hate and some calls for violence against you. You have felt your voices had the power of truth. Now, you tell me they have sent you a warning. I had prayed that the powers that gave you this mission would protect and not sacrifice you. My prayers have been answered and now they seek to protect you. Do not hesitate. Heed that warning and escape the wrath of those that hate you." Joseph shook his head. I don't know what to do. I am not a coward. I am prepared to stand my ground." Allison replied, "No. You must leave at once. Go to your father he is wise and loves you and will advise you correctly. He will help decide what is best for you." Joseph thought and then said, "I will go only if you come with me. Life without you is not worth living."

"Gladly, I am so happy you asked me. We must leave now."

Joseph said, "Good, I will pick you up in twenty minutes. I will call my Dad and let him know we are coming." He made his call and also told his roommate Jack, he was leaving because there was a threat on his life and would be going to his parents but not to divulge his location to anyone. Jack assured him he would respect that confidence and expressed his best wishes. Thirty minutes later, having picked up Allison they were on their way to his parents' home.

The drive to his parents home was lengthy and they did nor arrive until very late at night. As they drove into the driveway, his father was outside waiting. He greeted Joseph with great warmth, hugging and kissing him and he expressed his pleasure that Allison was with him. After greeting his mother and comfortably seated in the living room, Joseph couldn't help expressing his wonder at the warmth of his father's greeting. Jokingly he said, "Dad, you greeted me as though I was returning from the dead." His father looking grim and serious said, "Joseph, that is no joke, I had real fears for your safety. Let me give you some bad news, I had a call from your roommate Jack. He called me not from your phone, but a pay phone." Joseph puzzled said, "What's going on? Has something bad happened?"

"Yes, two masked men broke into your room and demanded your whereabouts. They were armed and had planned to kill you. Jack denied knowing your specific whereabouts and said you might have gone to a nightclub at the beach. They left frustrated and angry. Jack made a call from a non-traceable public phone to warn us." Shocked by this news Joseph and Allison congratulated themselves on the action they had taken. Then Joseph explained the cause of their fortunate escape by relating the dream he had experienced and the benefit they had received by taking its warning seriously. He told his parents that it was Allison who had really persuaded him to take it seriously and go to his parents. The parents expressed their heartfelt gratitude to Allison.

His father then said, "Joseph, I don't know what to make of these voices that rule you and give you warning except that they are proven correct and appear to be protecting you. Now you must plan on a way of life that will defeat the aim of those hate mongers who seek your death. You cannot stay here. This is the first place they will look for you. You must change your name and register tonight at a motel with your new name. Allison will stay here just for tonight. After tonight, you must leave for an undisclosed location where you can achieve oblivion and anonymity. I will have you set up with an individual, not a relative, through whom we can maintain contact and handle affairs without the risk of outside discovery. I will be able to provide you with sufficient cash to susidize you for a year after which our secret contact will be able to provide as needed. After you leave, I feel we should have three months of no contact except for emergencies, and that only through our secret contact. We are dealing here with life and death and must take every precaution." Joseph spoke to his father, "Dad, I agree with everything you said and the wisdom you display, I have only one condition. I know my life is at stake, but I don't want to go into permanent hiding without Allison.If she will agree, I want to marry her and take her as my wife into this barren future. She is my life and without her there would be no living." Joseph's father looked at Allison, who smiled and said, "If this is an official proposal of marriage, I accept." The Father exclaimed, "Fine, I will arrange a marriage ceremony here at our home in the morning. You will be married under your new name, which we will select, now. Allison, with your permission and assistance, we will compose a message to your parents, which I will transmit by a non-traceable phone call. I will set up a Post Office box that they can send messages to you that I will insure you receive. Following your marriage you will both leave for an undisclosed location. A rented car will be at your disposal, rented by someone else. It can be returned near your new location and a new car purchased under your new name. Your appearance should be altered, perhaps growing a beard could help, with sun glasses, and face garb." Now we should select a name and a place for you to live. The name should be a common one that ceates problems in tracing." They decided on William Smith. And Allison would become Alice Smith. The father said, "I think that covers everything we can do tonight. I will do research tomorrow and select a small remote village where you can settle until things quiet down and your name disappears from publi.interest. Is there anything further we should do?" Joseph spoke up. I need to communicate with Professor Williams and explain wha is going on. How can I communicate with him?" His father thought and then said, "I will give you a cell phone and will have that number given to Professor Williams by a not connected friend to have him call you. Cell phones cannot be tapped." Since the hour was quite late, they decided to call it a night, Joseph left for his motel. Allison was given a room and prepared for sleep as did Joseph's parents.

The next morning, Joseph checked out of the motel and headed for his parents residence where he joined his mother and Allison for breakfast. His father had left early to busily arrange the morning's doings. About ten A.M., Joseph's cell phone rang. It was Professor Williams calling. Joseph related all the events leading to his sudden departure. The heeded dream warning, the following attempt on his life and his and Allison's plan to go into hiding and disappear from the public view. Professor Williams gave his wholehearted approval of his actions. He said, "Joseph, you have fulfilled your mission amd accomplished its purpose. Your presence is no longer relevant since it would only result in your permanent removal. You have established truths that must be recognized and dealt with. I want you to know that your message shall not be put aside and forgotten. I plan to organize a following that will press ahead with a program to stop our path of self-detruction, I will be working with a Senator Frank Duncan, who supports your views and will present them to Congress for discussion. There are other groups who accept the truths of your message and will work with us to bring them into the public arena. Whether the human race can change from 'destructive to productive' behavior is a moot question that only time can resolve.but we, the concerned, need to make the effort. Now, accept my desire for your happiness with your true love and my thanks for opening the window of reality to the true status of our condition. If possible, would like to maintain communication with you." Joseph thanked him for his good wishes and his past support and kindness. He agreed with the desire to maintain contact and gave him the post office box number that would enable him to keep Joseph posted on event happenings. Although, Joseph might not be able to reply. With that understanding their phone conversation ended.

A short time later, the father appeared with a civic official and a marriage license that would unite William Smith and Alice Kimberly in marriage. After the marriage ceremony they sat at the kitchen table. Mr.Stern spread a large map on the table and pointed to a tiny village in Oregon with the name of Placerville. Here he said is an ideal town for you to take refuge in. It has a population of nine hundred with pratically no outside contacts. The people are addicted to old traditional ways and disapprove of newspapers, radio and television. Homes are extremely cheap and you should buy a house to avoid landlord inquirys. Now, you must leave and put the necessary miles between us. Joseph got up and with tears expressed his love as he hugged his father and kissed a weeping mother. Allison also was hugged and kissed and then bundled into their car they left leaving the disconsolate parents behind them.

CHAPTER 9

▼

Several months later, Joseph and Allison were comfortable in their new surroundings. They had established good relations with the villagers and had not been disturbed by any recognition or inquirys. Joseph had grown a beard so that identification was less of a threat. There happiness with each other and their interest in the beautiful forests, gardening and outside interests help protect them from some of the frustration of being so isolated from world information and activity. On this particular day, Joseph was delighted to receive a mailed package. The package contained information assembled by Professor Williams. There also was a brief note from him. Joseph, it read, I wanted you read this news item of Senator Frank Duncan's presentation to congress. Perhaps it will encourage you to feel that your message has been heard. I have been active with an organization that has acquired a respectable number of members. We are pursuing the promotion of your message. You and your wife are in my thoughts and look forward to the day when your isolation will end and we can reestablish our personal relationship. Now enjoy Senator Frank Duncan's speech. Finishing Professor Williams's note, Joseph picked up and read the Senator's speech to congress.

The Senator spoke, "Members of Congress, at this opening meeting of our legislative session, I would like to present some new thoughts and ideas that may affect our legislation. These new thoughts were first presented, as you undoubtedly heard, by a Joseph Stern, whom some classified as a prophet. What he claimed, not as a prophet, was the recognition of existing truths. He did, in the end, prophecies that violations of these truths would end in extermination of the human race. What are these truths that humans violate that will bring destruction? First category: violations of the laws of the universe and nature such as-Murdering their own species: Poisoning air, water and land:Overpopulation beyond the planet's capacity: depletion of natural resources: Second category-Human behavior that violates laws of society such as-Condoning the rule of dictators: religious beliefs that preach love and practice hate: Beliefs that teach life is only preparation for death: Condoning the murder of innocents in religious and racist killings: Allowing irresponsible rulers to develop weapons of mass destruction: Beliefs that heavenly powers will protect man from his own misbehavior and destruction. Many will argue these are merely opinions that the future will change and should not be taken seriously. The answer is-Are these truth existing NOW? Will the future really change human behavior? Only by accepting the fact that it is now that requires immediate corrective action and not some future hope for miracle can we stem the threatening flood. I urge the congress to take seriously this message brought by Joseph Stern, perhaps from heavenly sources, and begin to reverse the destructive direction of our present course. As the most powerful nation on this planet, we have a duty to do this.

"Let us fulfill our responsibility. Thank you." He sat with the sound of loud applause." Joseph finished. He had been reading it to Allison, his voice choking at times with emotion. Allison reached and took his hand. Joseph said through tears, "Strange, I feel rewarded. I am the happiest man. I once told you in an outburst I couldn't control, that I wanted to change the world. I didn't think, I could. I still think that I can't. But now I feel I have started something. And I believe one person can change the world."

THE END

978-0-595-40095-9
0-595-40095-7

Printed in the United States
63390LVS00003B/169-225